"It's dark, friend, and I've got a gun pressed to the lady's back, don't I, miss? Tell him!"

"Yes, he does!" Honey blurted.

"Okay," Clint said, "so now what?"

"Now nothing," the man said. "I made a mistake. I'm going to back out of here and be on my way. Don't follow or I'll kill the woman."

"No good, friend," Clint said. "You're not taking her with you."

"I'll kill her!"

"And then I'll kill you . . ."

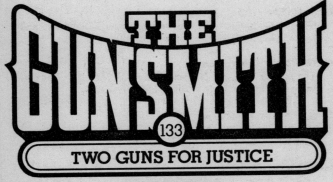

THE GUNSMITH

133

TWO GUNS FOR JUSTICE

J. R. ROBERTS

JOVE BOOKS, NEW YORK

TWO GUNS FOR JUSTICE

A Jove Book / published by arrangement with
the author

PRINTING HISTORY
Jove edition / January 1993

ISBN: 0-515-11020-5

Jove Books are published by The Berkley Publishing Group,
200 Madison Avenue, New York, New York 10016.
The name "JOVE" and the "J" logo
are trademarks belonging to Jove Publications, Inc.

PRINTED IN THE UNITED STATES OF AMERICA

10 9 8 7 6 5 4 3 2 1

ONE

Hammer was the first one to see the smoke.

"See it?" he said to Clint Adams. He was pointing due north.

Clint strained his eyes and thought he saw a tendril of white smoke rising toward the sky.

"You have the eyes of an Indian," Clint said to Hammer. This observation was unsurprising since Fred Hammer had spent so many of his formative years among Indians.

"We'd better take a look," Hammer said.

Clint and Hammer had met up a week earlier, purely by accident. They had worked together many times in the past, and had even come to think of each other as friends. This time they both had been riding through Nevada and had stopped in the same town about an hour apart. Neither of them believed in coincidence, so when Hammer walked into the same saloon where Clint was playing poker, they were faced with a problem. Was this coincidence, or the workings of some higher intelligence?

● ● ●

1

Clint had been doing very well in a low-stakes poker game when he saw Hammer walk in. Everyone else saw him, too. The black man was hard to miss. He stood nearly six four or five with hardly any waist to speak of. He wore a flat-brimmed black hat, black shirt, and black pants. He was not a man to go unnoticed. Clint knew that the saloon girls in the place were especially noticing him.

Hammer walked to the bar, ordered a beer, then turned to survey the room. If he saw Clint Adams he did not let it show.

Clint finished the hand and cashed out of the game. He walked to the bar, stood next to Hammer, and ordered a beer.

"Fancy seeing you here," Hammer said, still not looking at Clint.

"What brings you through here?" Clint asked.

Hammer shrugged and said, "Just drifting. You?"

"Same thing."

The word "coincidence" hung in the air between them, but neither would use it.

They decided to ride out together and not discuss it any further.

"Somebody's in trouble," the big black man said now, with assurance.

"We'd better go and check, then," Clint said.

They rode toward the thin swirl of smoke.

They both saw the overturned wagon at the same time, and Clint put his hand out to stop Hammer from riding to it.

"Let's wait a minute," he said.

"Might be somebody still alive down there," Hammer said.

"They can wait a few minutes more," Clint said. "That's better than riding into some kind of a trap."

"A trap set by who?" Hammer asked, frowning. "Nobody knew we were coming this way."

"I'm not saying it's a trap set especially for us," Clint said. "Could be for anyone."

"I think you're letting your legend go to your head," Hammer said. He often teased Clint about his Gunsmith legend. Of course, that was only because Hammer knew the man *behind* the legend. "You're seeing traps where there are none."

"I tell you what," Clint said. "You go ahead and ride on up to that wagon, and I'll cover you from here."

"Wait a minute," Hammer said. "Why should *I* ride up to it and you stay here and cover me? Why don't *you* ride down and *I'll* cover *you*?"

"Because *you're* the one who doesn't believe in traps," Clint said.

"I didn't say I *didn't* believe in them," Hammer said, hedging, "I just said I didn't see them everywhere."

"Well," Clint said, "I don't see one here, but let's just ride in a circle for a few minutes."

They circled the overturned wagon, which is where the white smoke was coming from. It was no longer on fire, but it had been not long ago.

As they circled the scene they spotted several bodies lying outside the wagon. Once they had made a complete circle around it they concluded that there was no trap.

"See?" Hammer said as they rode down to the wagon.

"That's what I like about you, Hammer," Clint said. "You never say 'I told you so.'"

"Sure I do," Hammer said, "when I'm right."

"That's what I mean," Clint said, "*never*."

TWO

Despite the fact that they had inspected the area, they still exercised caution in approaching the wagon.

"I'll check the wagon," Clint said, as they dismounted.

Hammer nodded and proceeded to inspect the three bodies that were on the ground.

Clint looked inside the wagon, half of which was charred black. The contents of the wagon also had been badly burned, beyond any salvaging.

That is, everything but the man.

"Jesus," Clint said. He leaned into the wagon to get a better look. It was a man, all right, a *young* man, and he didn't appear to be badly burned. In fact, Clint suspected that he hadn't been in the wagon at all while it had been burning, but had probably crawled into it later, possibly to hide.

Clint looked closer, then stepped one foot into the wagon and saw that the man's chest was rising and falling.

"Hammer?"

"They're all dead, Clint," Hammer called back. "Three men, all dead. Shot."

"I got one here," Clint said, climbing into the wagon, "and he's alive. Give me a hand."

Hammer hurried over and peered into the wagon. Clint grabbed the man beneath his arms and Hammer reached in to take his legs. Together they lifted him from the wagon and laid him on the ground.

"Get some water," Clint said.

Hammer hurried to his saddle for his canteen. Clint leaned over the young man and checked him for injuries. He appeared to have been beaten, but didn't seem otherwise injured. There was a gash on his head that had bled and then crusted over. There was no portion of his body that was burned, leading Clint to put credence in his initial assumption, that the man had crawled into the wagon *after* it had burned.

Hammer returned with the water. Clint lifted the man's head and held the canteen to his mouth. When the water touched the man's mouth he seemed to come instantly awake and started to swallow anxiously.

"Easy," Clint said, taking the canteen away, "not too much."

Clint took his neckerchief off, wet it, and cleaned the man's face. Both he and Hammer were now able to see that the man was hardly more than a boy, nineteen or twenty years old, if that.

"Can you sit up?"

"I-I think so," the man said.

With Clint's assistance he did so.

"What happened?" he asked.

"That's what we were going to ask you," Clint said. "We just found you here."

The youngster looked around him, frowning.

"Can you tell us what happened?" Hammer asked.

He looked up at the big black man, seeing him for the first time, and his eyes widened momentarily.

"I—I can't seem to remember," he said, finally.

"Let's start with something easy, then," Clint said. "What's your name?"

The young man thought a moment, his brow furrowing mightily, and then he shook his head and said, "I can't seem to remember that, either."

Clint looked at Hammer, who shrugged.

"Well," Clint said, "we'd better get you to a doctor, then. Can you stand?"

"If you help me."

Clint and Hammer helped the man to his feet. He became dizzy at first, needing their assistance to remain standing, and finally was able to stand on his own. It was then he saw the bodies on the ground.

"Jesus," he said, "did—did I do that?"

"We don't know," Clint said.

The man turned and looked at the burned-out wagon.

"Was I in there?"

"Yes," Clint said.

He looked down at himself and said, "I'm not burned."

"I think you crawled into it after it burned," Clint said. "Probably for shelter."

"Or to hide," Hammer said.

"Hide?" the man asked. "From who?"

"I don't know," Hammer said.

"Certainly not from these men," Clint said, "but maybe there were others."

"I-I don't—I can't remember—" the man said, holding his head.

"Do you know any of these men?" Hammer asked. He had turned them over to check them, and they were all lying on their backs. They each had been shot.

The young man studied their faces for a few moments, then shook his head and said, "I-I don't think I know them."

"Come on," Clint said, putting his hand on the man's shoulder, "the faster we get you to a doctor the quicker you'll start to remember what happened. You can ride double with me. There's bound to be a town farther on."

They moved to Clint's horse. He mounted first and then Hammer helped the other man climb on behind him. He was slightly built and no hardship at all for Clint's big black gelding, Duke, to carry.

"Maybe I'd better look through the wagon for something salvageable," Hammer suggested.

Clint frowned. He didn't know if his friend wanted to salvage something for the young man, or scavenge something for himself.

"It's burned out pretty badly, Hammer," Clint said. "Let's just get this fella to a doctor."

Hammer gave the wagon a last look, then said, "All right," and mounted up.

THREE

The town they came to was called Taylor, Nevada, and while not a big town it certainly was of a size that would have to have a local doctor.

As they entered town and rode down the main street Hammer attracted a lot of attention. Clint took the opportunity to stop a citizen who was crossing the street—and staring at Hammer—and asked where the doctor's office was. He received directions and thanked the man, who continued on his way—and continued staring at Hammer.

"Jesus," Hammer said, "you'd think they never saw a black man before."

The doctor's office was right on the main street, so they rode directly to it. Hammer dismounted first, then helped the injured man down from behind Clint. Clint then dismounted and, propping the man between them, they entered the office.

The doctor was a tall, angular man in his fifties who responded immediately when they entered the office.

"Bring him over here," he said, indicating a padded examination table. The office was one room, but there was a curtain separating the table from the rest of the room. "What happened to him?"

"We're not sure, Doc," Clint said, "and he can't seem to remember."

The doctor was already examining him, looking at the gash on his head and into his eyes.

"With this head wound it's no wonder he can't remember," the doctor said. "Is he a friend of yours?"

"We just found him, Doc, is all," Hammer said.

"All right, then," the doctor said, "both of you get out and let me do my job. You can come back in a little while and maybe I'll have something to tell you—if you're interested, that is."

"We're interested, Doc," Clint said. "We'll be back in about half an hour."

"That's fine," the doctor said. "In the meantime you might want to go and see the sheriff. He likes to know what's going on in town."

"We'll stop in and see him," Clint promised.

"*You* stop in and see the sheriff," Hammer said. "I don't like lawmen. I'll go and get a drink."

"Take my horse, will you? I'll join you at the saloon after I talk to him."

"Right."

Outside they separated, Hammer walking both horses as he searched for a saloon, and Clint in quest of the sheriff's office. It wasn't hard to locate, as it was also situated on the main street.

Clint knocked on the office door and then opened it and entered. There was a man standing at a pot-bellied stove, pouring himself a cup of coffee. He was about the doctor's age, as tall but heavier through the shoulders and chest. He was hatless in the office, and

Clint could see that there was a ring of graying dark hair surrounding a gleaming, bald pate. As if to make up for the lack of hair on his head the man had the biggest mustache Clint had ever seen. It covered his entire upper lip and swept out in long, waxed tips.

"Can I help you?" the man asked.

"Are you the sheriff?"

The man's body had been half turned, and as he faced Clint, the badge on his chest came into view.

"That's right," he said, "Sheriff Tom Ridge. Just get into town?"

"That's right," Clint said, "my partner and I." He went on to explain how they had come to find the injured man and to transport him into town.

"Three dead men, did you say?"

"That's right."

"And this jasper claims he can't remember anything?" the sheriff asked. His disbelief was plain on his face.

"That's right."

"He's probably lying."

"You think he killed those three men and then injured himself? And now he's claiming not to remember anything?"

"I just don't like the convenience of not remembering anything," the lawman said, putting his coffee cup down on his desk. "He's over at the Doc Fraley's, you say?"

"That's right," Clint said, "if that's the doctor's name. We didn't have time to get formally introduced. I'll be going back over there in about half an hour to see how he is."

"This fella a friend of yours?" The sheriff picked up his hat and set it carefully on his head.

"Like I told you before," Clint said, "we just found him."

"A stranger, then."

"That's right," Clint said, "but that doesn't mean we're not interested in how he's doing."

"Well, I better get over there and check on his story," the sheriff said. "By the way, you and your partner got names?"

"My name's Clint Adams," Clint said, "and he's Fred Hammer."

"Adams, huh?" the sheriff said.

"Yeah, that's right."

Clint thought the man recognized the name, but if he did he wasn't saying.

"Well, Mr. Adams, what are your plans now?"

"Right now I plan to have a drink, then check back with the doctor."

"Staying in town?"

"Probably overnight."

"Well then, we'll talk again later."

"Sure," Clint said, "anytime."

They left the office together and the sheriff nodded to him and started over to the doctor's office. Clint hoped he let the injured man recover to some extent before he started interrogating him.

FOUR

Clint found Hammer standing at the bar of Taylor's only saloon. The black man had a beer in his hand and the mug was only half full. It was mid-afternoon and there were some other customers in the place, all of whom were finding Hammer very interesting.

Clint approached the bar and said to the bartender, "A beer."

"Comin' up."

"Talk to the sheriff?" Hammer asked.

"Yeah," Clint said, "his name's Ridge, Tom Ridge. Ever hear of him?"

"No, can't say I have," Hammer said. "He hear of you?"

"I think so."

"Didn't let on, huh?"

"No."

"What'd he say?"

"He's going over to the doctor's office to talk to . . . to whoever that is we brought in."

"John," Hammer said, "let's call him John."

"Sure," Clint said, "John."

13

"Ain't he gonna let the poor guy recover before he starts questioning him?"

"I don't think so," Clint said. "Seems the sheriff doesn't believe that, uh, John can't remember what happened."

"He made that decision already? Jumping to conclusions, ain't he?"

"I guess," Clint said as the bartender put his beer down on the bar.

"We stayin' the night?"

"Makes sense," Clint said. "I'd like to make sure the kid is all right before we leave."

"Be nice to find out who he is and what happened." Hammer said. "I'm the nosy sort, you know."

"Curious," Clint said, "not nosy, and yeah, I agree. Let's finish these beers and get settled at the hotel before we go back to the doctor's office."

They drank their beers and left the saloon. First they took the horses to the livery stable and then walked over to the hotel. They were able to get two rooms with no trouble and stow their gear before starting over to the doctor's again.

When they entered the office the sheriff was still there, waiting around. The curtain was closed, so Clint assumed that the doctor was still examining "John."

"Sheriff, this is Fred Hammer."

The sheriff nodded to Hammer and looked him over frankly.

"Too many people in here," Hammer said. "I'll take a turn around town. You let me know what happens."

"You're friend the nervous type?" Ridge asked.

"Hardly," Clint said. "He just doesn't like crowds."

"Hmmm," Ridge said. "Seems I've seen him somewhere before."

"He's got one of those faces," Clint said. "Did you get a chance to talk to John yet?"

"John?" Ridge said, frowning. "I thought you didn't know his name?"

"We just decided to call him that," Clint said. "It's better than nothing."

"Oh," Ridge said, looking like he thought something was being pulled on him. "Well, I talked to him briefly, but the Doc is still checking on him."

At that moment the curtain was pulled back and the doctor stepped out. He turned his back to them and very deliberately pulled the curtain closed again.

"Doc, can I talk to him now?" the sheriff asked.

"No," Doc Fraley said, and then looked at Clint and said, "and neither can you. Nobody is going to talk to him until tomorrow. He's too disoriented to make any sense, anyway."

"How badly is he hurt?" Clint asked.

"Aside from the gash on his head he seemed to have been beaten," the doctor said.

"And he still claims he can't remember what happened?" the sheriff asked.

"He doesn't claim it, Tom," Doc Fraley said, "I think and note he really does have amnesia."

"Am—what?" the sheriff asked.

"Amnesia," the doctor said. "It's a condition whereby the person can't remember anything about his past. I've read about it."

"But you've never seen a case of it before?" the sheriff asked.

"No."

"Then you can't be sure he's not faking."

"Tom, he's got a bump and a swelling on his head," the doctor said. "I doubt that he's faking."

"I still have to talk to him, Doc," the sheriff said. "There's the question of three dead men to answer."

"Well, why don't you go and collect your three dead men," the doctor said. "Maybe *that'll* tell you something, and you can talk to my patient tomorrow."

Ridge frowned and said, "Yeah, well . . . I'll have someone go out there with me and pick them up. I'll want you to look at them, Doc."

"That's part of my job."

"And I want to talk to this fella first thing in the morning."

"You'll be able to do that," the doctor said, his tone reassuring. Clint thought that the doctor knew just how to handle the lawman.

The sheriff nodded, apparently satisfied, and left the office.

"Sticks to his opinions, doesn't he?" Clint said.

"He's stubborn, all right," the doctor said, "but he's a good man. Can I do something else for you, sir?"

"Clint Adams, Doc," Clint said, sticking his hand out.

"Otis Fraley," the doctor said, shaking hands.

"You going to keep him here overnight?" Clint asked.

"Yes, I want to keep an eye on him."

"All right, then," Clint said. "We're over at the hotel if you need us for anything."

"Very good," the doctor said.

"Has he remembered his name yet, Doc?"

"Nothing," the doctor said, "nothing at all, Mr. Adams. If he does remember something, I'll send for you *and* for the sheriff."

"I understand," Clint said. "All right, Doc, thank you. See you in the morning."

"We'll be here," the doctor said.

Clint shook the man's hand again and then left the office to find Hammer.

FIVE

True to his word Hammer was taking a walk around town. Clint caught up to him and matched the big black man's long strides.

"I don't like that sheriff," Hammer said.

"You don't like *any* lawman," Clint said.

"That's true. I didn't like the way *this* one was looking at me, though."

"He said you were familiar," Clint said. "There's no, uh, paper out on you anywhere, is there, Hammer?"

"Hell, no, Clint," Hammer said. "Those days are gone for me. I make my fortunes on the up and up now."

"I can see that," Clint said. "What do you say we get something to eat?"

"Sounds good to me."

"You pass anyplace that looked interesting in your travels?"

"I just might have," Hammer said. "Let's see if I can remember . . ."

Hammer took Clint to a small café, the type that most towns give birth to. People who don't want to

18

eat in the hotel dining rooms, and who aren't satisfied with saloon fare, will usually frequent small
cafés like this one. There were about ten or twelve
tables, and it was run by a husband and wife, both
of whom looked like they sampled their own food
often.

"What's good?" Clint asked the wife, who was
acting as waitress.

She touched her round belly and said, "Can't you
tell? Everything!"

"Your husband does the cooking?" Clint asked.

"On Tuesdays, Thursdays, and Saturdays," she
said.

"That means you cook on Mondays, Wednesdays,
and Fridays?" he asked.

"Right."

"Who cooks on Sundays?" Hammer asked.

"We both do," she said.

"What's your husband's best dish?" Clint asked.

"Stew."

Why did small cafés like this one usually special-
ize in stew? he wondered. Was it because it was easy
to make a lot of it?

"I'll have the stew," he said.

"Me, too."

"Comin' up," she said.

"And coffee," Clint said.

"Before or after?"

"Both," he said, and she nodded, all of her cheeks
waggling.

"So what do you think?" Hammer asked.

"About what?"

"About our friend, John. Think he really can't
remember?"

"The doctor thinks he's telling the truth."

"And the sheriff thinks he's lying," Hammer said.

"That's the sheriff's job," Clint said. "We should know more tomorrow morning."

"We should be *leaving* tomorrow morning," Hammer said.

"And we will," Clint said, "*after* we find out what really happened."

"Curious?"

"Aren't you?" Clint asked. "Did he kill three men and then forget? If so, where's his gun? He didn't have one on him, and we didn't find any other than the ones on the dead men—*and their guns were still in their holsters.* Somebody killed them before they had a chance to clear leather. Do you think it was him?"

"Couldn't have been," Hammer said. "He's just a kid, and not only didn't he have a gun, but he didn't have a gunbelt on."

"All of which makes me curious," Clint said.

"So okay," Hammer said, "we'll wait long enough to find out if he remembers anything or not, but if he doesn't we leave—at least, *I'll* leave. I'm not going to hang around here any longer than I have to."

"Did we talk about where you're headed when we met up?" Clint asked.

"Just drifting," Hammer said, "until something comes along."

The woman came back with their coffee and poured them each a cup.

"Just him," Hammer said. "I only have one cup, and that's after dinner."

"I'm sorry," she said, reaching for the second cup to dispose of it.

"Leave it," Clint said, "I'll drink it."

"I'll be right out with your food."

"You know," Hammer said, "the way I figure it those three jaspers tried to rob this fella, and got one helluva big surprise."

"But not from him, right?"

Hammer shook his head.

"Couldn't be," Hammer said. "I guess I *am* curious, now that you mention it."

She came back with their stew and they dug in, finding it delicious. After dinner she brought more coffee, and then presented them with the bill. As they had been doing all along, they split it.

"Let's hit the saloon," Hammer said. "I could use a drink, a card game, and a girl—not necessarily in that order."

Clint couldn't think of an argument against any of the three.

SIX

"Hey, the sheriff's bringin' in some bodies," somebody yelled.

Clint was standing at the bar nursing a beer, and Hammer was involved in a poker game. The black man looked up at the sound of the voice, and Clint put his beer mug down on the bar and walked to the front doors to take a look outside. He had to elbow his way through some of the other patrons who were trying to get a look.

Sure enough the sheriff was riding down the street on horseback. Behind him was a man on a buckboard, and in the back of the buckboard were the bodies of the three dead men Clint and Hammer had found.

Clint turned to look back inside at Hammer, who nodded that he understood that Clint was going to step outside. There were many others watching the scene as well, but their watching was just a morbid curiosity. Clint wanted to find out if the sheriff had recognized any of the three men when he collected them.

He started walking down the street, keeping the

buckboard in sight until it stopped in front of the undertaker's office. At that point he quickened his pace and crossed the street. He reached the sheriff just as he was dismounting.

"Sheriff," he said, "I see you found them with no problem."

The sheriff dismounted and turned to face Clint. He didn't seem surprised to see him there.

"I found them, Mr. Adams," the lawman said.

The man who dropped down from the buckboard seat was wearing a deputy's badge. He was a good-looking young man in his late twenties.

"What should I do now, Sheriff?" he asked.

"Go inside and ask Ed where he wants us to put these bodies," the sheriff said.

"Did you get a good look at the men, Sheriff?" Clint asked.

"I did, yeah."

"Know them?"

"No, Mr. Adams, I don't know them," he said. "Would you like to take another look at them? Maybe *you'll* recognize them."

"Sure," Clint said, "anything to help."

They walked to the back of the buckboard where Clint took a good look at the three men.

"No," he said, finally, "I don't recognize any of them."

"But these are the three men you found out there," the sheriff said. "I haven't gone and found three *other* dead men."

"Oh, no," Clint said, "these are them, all right, Sheriff."

"All of these men still had their guns," the sheriff commented.

"I know that," Clint said. "I noticed that when we found them."

"Whoever killed them must have been real good with a gun," the sheriff said. "None of them were shot in the back, they were all facing their killer."

"That's interesting."

"It sure is."

The sheriff studied Clint for a few moments and Clint knew then for sure that the sheriff knew who he was. He also knew what the man was thinking—that the Gunsmith might have been able to gun down three men before any of them could clear their guns.

At that point the undertaker, Ed Block, came out to take a look at the bodies. He was an ordinary looking man in his forties, one who could just as well have been a bartender or a storekeeper.

"Do you know any of these men, Ed?" the sheriff asked him.

The undertaker took a moment to study them, then shook his head.

"Can't say I do, Sheriff."

"Where do you want them?" Ridge asked.

"Just bring them inside, Sheriff."

Ridge turned to Clint, who for a moment thought the man was going to ask him to help.

"If you'll excuse me, Mr. Adams," he said, "I have to get these bodies inside, and then bring the doctor over to have a look at them."

"Sure, Sheriff," Clint said, moving clear. "If you need to talk to me again, I'll be at the saloon."

"Is Hammer there?"

"Yes," Clint said, "Hammer's over there, too."

"I'm sure we *will* need to talk again," Ridge said,

sternly. "I'll probably come over there when I'm finished here."

"Fine," Clint said, "Hammer's playing poker, but I'll buy you a beer."

Clint left them as Ridge and his deputy were easing one of the bodies off the back of the buckboard. He was starting to think that if the sheriff was going to suspect him of killing these men it might be a good idea for him and Hammer to leave town as soon as possible. He didn't need for his reputation to get him into trouble when he hadn't even *touched* a gun.

Clint went back to the saloon and to his beer. The bartender, when he entered, dumped the beer he had left and supplied him with a fresh one.

"Thanks," Clint said.

"Sure."

Hammer excused himself from the game for one round and came to the bar for a beer.

"Talk to the man?" he asked Clint.

"The sheriff doesn't know the dead men."

"He ask about me?"

"Just if you were over here," Clint said, "but he's starting to look at *me* funny because the men were all killed with their guns still in their holsters."

"I didn't notice any of them bein' backshot," Hammer said.

"They weren't."

Hammer picked up his beer and said, "Then I can see why he's lookin' at you funny. Better you than me."

"Thanks."

"I guess you'd like to get an early start in the morning?"

Clint thought a moment and then said, "Maybe, but I don't want it to look like we're running, either."

"Well, since you're the one he's lookin' at funny, you call the play," Hammer said. "I got to get back to my game."

"He might be over here later."

"Fine," Hammer said, "you entertain him and keep him away from me."

"Why sure, Hammer," Clint said, "ain't that why I'm here?"

SEVEN

Clint had ordered another beer and had taken it to a corner table by the time the sheriff entered the saloon. The lawman stopped just inside the batwing doors and took a moment to look around. Clint could see that the man was an experienced lawman. He didn't walk into the room until he had checked it out completely, or until he had located everyone he wanted to locate. He knew that Hammer was at the poker table, and he saw Clint in the back, and only *then* did he approach the bar and order a beer. Armed with the full mug he walked over to Clint's table.

"Have a seat," Clint said.

The lawman sat.

"I thought I recall saying I was going to buy you a beer," Clint said.

"That's all right," Ridge said, "I can buy my own beer."

Clint had not seen any money change hands at the bar, but he didn't comment on it.

"Get those three fellas taken care of?"

"Yes," Ridge said. "The doctor did his job, and now the undertaker will do his."

27

"The Doc recognize any of them as an old patient?" Clint asked.

"No."

"Looks like you got three strangers on your hands."

"Three *dead* strangers," the sheriff said. He turned in his seat to look at Hammer, and then turned back. "I've still got two live ones to worry about."

"Three," Clint said, "counting our friend with the lost memory."

"Oh, yeah," Ridge said, "him."

"You still don't believe he's lost his memory, do you?" Clint asked.

Ridge made a face and said, "I guess I'm just naturally suspicious."

"Comes with the job," Clint said.

"That's right," Ridge said, "you *were* a lawman years ago, weren't you?"

"Years ago," Clint said, "and for a lot of years."

"Then you must know what my job is in this situation, right?"

"To suspect all strangers of murder?"

"It's not quite that cut and dried," Ridge said, "but you have to admit that there aren't too many men who could kill three men without giving them a chance to touch their guns."

"There are a few."

"Unfortunately for you, I only see one—unless you tell me that your friend Hammer is as good with a gun as you are."

"He's not."

"Then that just leaves you."

"I didn't kill them," Clint said, "I found them."

"So you say."

"So does Hammer."

"He's your witness?"

"I don't think I need one."

"Maybe the Doc's patient will suddenly get his memory back tomorrow, huh?" the sheriff said. "Then he could clear the whole thing up."

"He just might."

"Why don't you and your friend, Hammer, just plan on staying around until he *does* clear the whole thing up."

"Are you telling me not to leave town, Sheriff?" Clint asked.

"I'm saying it might be a good idea if neither one of you did," Sheriff Ridge said. "At least not until I have some answers."

Clint stared at the man without answering.

"Do you have a problem with that?" the sheriff asked.

"I guess that pretty much depends on how long it takes," Clint said.

"That's going to depend on when your friend gets his memory back."

"He's not my friend."

"Well, you know him better than I do," Ridge said. He stood up, leaving his beer untouched on the table. "Maybe you could talk to him, Mr. Adams. Maybe *you* could get him to get his memory back."

"Why don't we just wait until morning and see what the doctor says?" Clint said.

Ridge shrugged and said, "I can work with that."

"Maybe *he* killed them all."

"Sure," Ridge said, "he looks like he could use a gun like the Gunsmith, right?"

"You never know, Sheriff," Clint said, "you just never know."

After the sheriff left, one of the saloon girls came over to pick up the sheriff's glass.

"Can I get you anything else, mister?" she asked.

Clint took a good look at her. She was in her mid-twenties, dark-haired, with creamy skin and small, nicely rounded breasts.

"I guess I could use another beer . . ."

"Honey," she said.

"I'm sorry?"

"That's my name," she said. "Honey."

"Honey," he said.

"I'll bring that other beer."

He smiled at her and said, "I'll wait right here."

EIGHT

Clint ran his hand over Honey's hip and down along the line of her thigh. She had a finely toned body with firm breasts and thighs, and incredible buttocks.

He slid his hand around to her ass now, stroking first one cheek and then the other . . .

It had been late when he left the saloon with Honey, and Hammer—who had expressed interest in finding a woman—was still playing poker. From the look of the stack of chips in front of him he was just doing too well to quit, even for a woman.

"Don't worry about your friend," Honey had told him as they left. "Michelle and Alice are ready to fight over him when he's ready to leave."

"I don't think they'll have to fight for him," Clint said.

"Why not?"

"Knowing Hammer, I think he'll just take both of them," he told her.

"Not me," she said, sliding her hand up his arm, "I don't like to share a man with anyone."

"That's good," he'd replied, "because I don't like sharing a woman."

Honey moved her legs now, spreading them a bit so that he could slide his hand down between her thighs, finding her with his fingers. She was wet and ready. They had only been together a few hours and already he knew that Honey was almost *always* wet and ready. Of course, she told him that was just with him, but he took that remark with a grain of salt. It was enough for him to know that she was here with him even though he had told her that he didn't ever pay for sex.

"Never?" she had asked.

"Never."

Her eyes had glittered when she licked her lips and said, "Now you've got me curious."

Later, when her curiosity had been satisfied she'd said, "Now I see why you don't pay for it. God, I *should* pay *you*. That was the best sex I've ever had."

He let another comment go without a remark. Whether she meant it or not he didn't care. He *knew* that she had enjoyed herself, and so had he. That was all he was ever after when he took a woman to bed with him.

He inserted one finger gently into her, moving it about until she moaned and pressed her butt back against him. He removed his finger and she spread her legs wider so he could slide his penis between her thighs and *into* her from behind.

"Oooh," she moaned, "umm, ooh that feels so good, just leave it there like that, Clint . . ."

They stayed like that a little while and then it was she who initiated something a little more energetic. She began sliding back and forth on him and he gently moved his hips and found her rhythm, matching it.

She sucked in her breath and reached behind for him, sliding one hand onto his buttocks. He moved his left hand around to brush her breasts, and then squeeze them in turn. Finally, he began to tweak her nipples as their tempo quickened and she hastily rolled over onto her knees. He moved with her so that they wouldn't break contact, and then he was on his knees behind her, holding her hips and driving into her from behind while she moaned and cried out, clutching at the bedposts. Her long hair was flying around as she tossed her head, and her body began to grow slick with perspiration. He slid one hand from her hip around to her stomach, pressing it flat against her and then pushing with his hand each time he drove into her. She cried out again and then he felt her body begin to shake and quiver uncontrollably. He felt his own explosion welling up inside of him and he just let it come . . .

In the morning when he woke up she was lying on her back with the sheet down to her waist. Her small, round breasts were firm even in repose, and her brown nipples were soft. He hardened them by leaning over and first licking them, and then sucking them. She reached for him sleepily, pulled him atop her, and opened her legs. He pierced her easily and swiftly, and they welcomed in the new day . . .

●   ●   ●

Clint left Honey in his hotel room after he got dressed to go down for breakfast. In the hall he walked to Hammer's door and put his ear against it. From inside he heard voices. Well, they weren't voices, exactly, but they *were* sounds and they were human—even if it was only *vaguely* human.

Smiling, Clint banged on the door. It swung open after a few moments and Hammer was glaring at him. The big man was buck naked, and his huge erection was a threatening presence.

"How about a little breakfast?" Clint asked, innocently.

"I'm a little busy right now," Hammer said, "as you can see."

He opened the door wider so Clint could see the two women—Michelle and Alice, from the saloon—on the bed. Both were naked and smiling. Michelle was the blonde with big, pear-shaped breasts and a pale triangle between her legs, while Alice was a willowy brunette with hardly any curves at all, but a wickedly sexy mouth that she was now licking. As busy as Clint had been all night with Honey, he felt himself reacting to the presence of the two women.

"Well, join me downstairs when you're done here, then," Clint said.

"I'll be there," Hammer said, "later!"

Clint hardly heard the last word for the sound of the slamming door.

NINE

It was almost an hour before Hammer finally appeared in the hotel dining room. Clint was starting on his third cup of coffee.

"How's the food?" Hammer asked, sitting across from Clint.

"Terrible," Clint said. "Have eggs, they can't totally ruin them."

Hammer ordered eggs, ham, potatoes, and biscuits and another pot of coffee.

"Worked up an appetite, huh?" Clint said.

Hammer smiled, revealing straight, white, well-cared-for teeth and said, "You know me. I always have an appetite . . . for a lot of things."

"Did you do well at the game last night?"

"*Very* well."

"I hope you didn't rub it in?"

"What? You mean me taking all them white men's money? You think I would rub that in?"

"We've got enough trouble without having some irate poker players on our trail."

"You and the sheriff had a talk last night in the saloon," Hammer said. "Want to tell me about it?"

"Oh, he just didn't think we should leave town until our 'friend' recovered his memory."

"Jesus," Hammer said, "who knows how long that could take?"

"The sheriff seems to think we might be able to persuade him to get it back quick."

"He still doesn't believe that the fella *can't* remember, huh?"

"I guess not."

"Well," Hammer said as the waitress appeared with his food, "after I finish eating we can mosey over to the doctor's office and see what the story is. Maybe he *will* get his memory back today and clear us, and we can leave."

"I've got news for you, *and* for the sheriff," Clint said. "We're leaving no matter what our injured friend has to say."

Hammer grinned and said, "I like the sound of that, Clint."

"Shut up and eat," Clint said. "We've wasted enough time this morning."

"*My* time wasn't wasted," Hammer said, shaking his head, "no sir . . ."

After breakfast they left the hotel and walked over to the doctor's office. When they entered the doctor looked up from his desk. The curtain was drawn across his examining area.

"Good morning, Doc," Clint said. "How's the patient doing?"

"As well as can be expected," the doctor said.

"What's that mean?" Hammer asked. "Can he remember anything, or what?"

"Some things," the doctor said. "He woke up with

his name, at least. I believe he'll recover his memory, oh, within the next day . . . or two . . . or it might be a week."

"A week?" Hammer said.

"Yes, but it shouldn't be much longer than that," the doctor assured them.

"Great," Hammer said.

"Can we talk to him?" Clint asked.

The doctor studied them for a moment, then said, "One of you can, yes. Which one is up to you."

"You do it," Hammer said to Clint. "He might be afraid of the big black man. I'll wait outside."

Clint didn't argue. Hammer left and Clint approached the curtain. He pushed it aside and entered, letting it close behind him. The space was cramped, taken up mostly by the examination table and the man on it.

"How are you doing?" Clint asked.

The young man turned his head and looked at Clint.

"I'll be doing a lot better when I can get off this table," the man said. "My back is killing me. I need a night in a real bed."

"That can probably be arranged," Clint said. "Do you remember me?"

"Sure," the man said, "you found me yesterday—was it yesterday?"

"Yep, yesterday," Clint said, realizing he had asked the wrong question. He wanted to know if the man remembered anything that had happened *before* the attack.

"Can you remember anything else?"

"Well, I know who I am," he said.

"And who is that?"

"Jack Wagner."

"Well, Jack Wagner, what else do you remember?"

"I can tell you it was real scary yesterday, not remembering even that," Wagner said, ignoring the question. "I never thought the day would come when I didn't remember my own name."

"It must have been strange," Clint said, "but what I'd like to know—"

He stopped short as Jack Wagner put his finger to his lips and shook his head. The man then mouthed "not here," shaking his head again.

Clint frowned, but nodded that he understood. For some reason the young man did not feel he could talk freely here. Abruptly, he sat up and swung his legs around to dangle over the side.

"Oooh, my back," he said, stretching. "Think I can get out of here now?"

"I don't know," Clint said. "I guess we'll have to ask the doctor that."

Clint turned and pulled the curtain completely open.

"Doc, your patient wants to know if he can leave," Clint said to the doctor.

Doctor Fraley got up from behind his desk and walked over to Wagner, who was still sitting up.

"Give me a few moments?" he said to Clint.

"Sure," Clint said, and the doctor pulled the curtain closed again.

Clint waited right there for about ten minutes and heard the doctor give Wagner a few simple instructions, and ask a few questions, and then the curtain was opened again.

"What about it, Doc?" Clint asked.

"Sure," Doc Fraley said, "I guess he can leave, but I wouldn't try to put him on a horse yet. Get him a room at the hotel, let him walk around town a bit. It might be good for his memory."

"Okay, Doc," Clint said, "whatever you say."

"Thank you very much, Doctor," Wagner said. He looked at Clint helplessly, and then said to both of them, "I'm afraid I don't have any money. It must have been stolen, I guess . . ."

"Wait outside and I'll take care of it," Clint said.

"I'll pay you back," Wagner said.

Clint doubted it, but felt responsible at least for the man's medical bill. He paid the doctor's fee and then went outside. Jack Wagner was in the act of stretching again, his arms extended directly overhead.

"What the hell was that all about?" Clint asked.

Wagner looked at Clint, then looked around them furtively.

"I remember everything, Mr. Adams," Wagner said, finally. "We have to find someplace where we can talk. I have a lot to tell you."

"All right," Clint said, "let me find my partner, and then we'll go for a walk."

"Your partner?"

"Hammer," Clint said, "the black man."

"Oh, him," Wagner said. "Do we really have to include him?"

"I'm afraid so," Clint said. "Anything you want to say to me you'll have to say to him, too."

Wagner thought that over a moment, then shrugged and said, "Oh well, I guess I don't have much of a choice. Okay, then, let's find him. I've got a story to tell you."

TEN

They found Hammer and introduced him to Jack Wagner. After that they kept walking until they were away from town, where they couldn't possibly be overheard. Wagner was winded from the exercise and sat down on a large, flat rock. Clint and Hammer remained standing, and waited for him to tell his story.

"My name's Jack Wagner," the young man said, "and I'm on my way to Sacramento, California, to collect a large inheritance."

"How large?" Hammer asked.

"Literally millions of dollars," Wagner said.

Hammer looked at Clint and said, "He got hit harder on the head than we thought."

"No, it's true," Wagner said. "My father was a very rich and powerful man in California."

"Was?" Clint said.

"He died several months ago," Wagner said.

"And where were you when he died?" Hammer asked.

"I left home a few years ago," Wagner said. "I didn't want any part of my father or his fortune."

40

"And now that he's dead you've changed your mind?" Hammer asked.

"Well . . . yes, but it's not the way it sounds."

"How is it, then?" the black man asked.

"I didn't like the *way* my father made his money, or the way he used it to manipulate people . . . and things like banks . . . and politicians."

"But now that he's dead—"

"Let him finish," Clint said.

Hammer looked at Clint and said, "Do you believe all of this? It's probably as true as his story about amnesia."

"That's true," Wagner said, "it's all true. I didn't remember anything until this morning, and now I remember that I *have* to get to Sacramento to collect my inheritance. I have to be there in three weeks."

"Why three weeks?"

"The notification of my father's death came to me late," Wagner said. "Since I left home I've been moving around, but I've been keeping in touch with my sister. She's the one who sent me word. She also told me that if I wasn't there in three weeks—on September fifth, when the will is to be read—I'll lose my entire inheritance."

"And who will get it?" Clint asked.

"I don't know," Wagner said. "All I know is that I'm *supposed* to get it. I don't know who does if I don't—but there are plenty of possibilities."

"And you think that one of those possibilities sent those men after you to try to make sure you don't get there in time."

"Yes!" Wagner said, triumphantly. "You understand!"

Clint looked at Hammer, who raised his hands and said, "Leave me out of this. I *still* don't buy this inheritance story."

"But it's true," Wagner said. "I can prove it."

"How?" Hammer asked.

"Make sure I get to Sacramento," Wagner said. "When I collect my inheritance I'll reward you—both of you."

"But we have to go all the way to California to find out," Hammer said. "No thanks."

"It's not that far," Clint said.

"What?" Hammer asked.

"California is not that far away, Hammer," Clint said. "After all, we're in Nevada."

"What if we get there and find out that he was lying?" Hammer asked.

"What have we lost?" Clint said. "You said yourself that you've been looking for something to do—and if it's true, there could be a lot of money in it for us."

Clint looked at Wagner, who jumped in and said, "A *lot* of money."

"How much is a lot?" Hammer asked.

Wagner looked at Clint, who nodded, and then the younger man said, "I'm sure I could pay you five thousand dollars each."

Clint looked at Hammer now with his eyebrows raised.

"Where else are you going to make five thousand dollars?" he asked. "Did you make that at poker last night? I doubt it."

"This is crazy," Hammer said. "If this jasper is lying, or just plain crazy, then we're going to California for nothing."

"Hey," Clint said, "I *like* California."

Wagner was watching them both expectantly, *eagerly* even, and Hammer finally said, "Okay—but there's a lot more I want to know."

"I agree with that," Clint said. He looked at Wagner and said, "We need to ask a lot of questions."

"Like what?"

"Well, for starters," Hammer said, "what happened yesterday? Who killed those three men before they could even clear leather?"

"I don't know," Jack Wagner said. "I still can't remember."

ELEVEN

"That's it," Hammer said. "Count me out."

"It's true!" Wagner said, coming off his rock in a hurry. "There are still things I can't remember—mostly about yesterday."

"Just about the incident?" Clint asked.

"No," Wagner said, "I don't remember yesterday at all, *or* the day before."

"What's the last thing you *do* remember?" Clint asked.

"I'm not sure . . . I was in a town called Cory . . . was that in Nevada? What's today, anyway?"

"It's August twenty-first," Clint said.

"What?" Wagner said, looking aghast. "I've lost an entire week?"

"I was wondering about that when you said you had to be in Sacramento in three weeks," Clint said. "You've only got about *two* weeks."

"A whole week," Wagner said, turning pale, "gone."

"Jesus . . ." Hammer said, shaking his head.

"What?" Clint asked.

"Nothing," Hammer said, "I'm just beginning to

believe him. Look at his face."

"Yeah, I know," Clint said. Jack Wagner looked truly horrified at the prospect of having lost a whole week of his life.

"Let's get him back to town so he can get some rest in a real bed," Clint said. "Maybe with some rest the past week will return."

"Yeah," Wagner said, "maybe, but we've got to get going. If I don't get to Sacramento in time—"

"You'll get there in time," Clint said, "but first there's something you're going to have to do for us."

"What?"

"You're going to have to tell the sheriff what happened yesterday," Hammer said, "and that we had nothing to do with it."

"But I told you," Wagner said, "I don't remember—"

"We know that, Jack," Clint said, "but he suspects me of having killed those men. You're going to have to tell him some kind of a story to get me off the hook, otherwise he won't let us leave town."

"I understand," Wagner said, "but what am I going to tell him?"

"I don't know," Clint said, "but we'll think of something. Come on, let's get back to town."

Instead of getting Wagner a room of his own Clint allowed him to use his room, and his bed. Once they had left Wagner in the room, sampling the bed, Clint and Hammer went back down to the hotel dining room and ordered a pot of coffee. It was too early to go to the saloon, which probably wasn't even open yet.

"So you believe this fella's story?" Hammer asked.

"I think I do, yeah," Clint said, "but there's a way we can check on it."

"You mean sending a telegram to Sacramento to ask about his father dying?"

"That's one way," Clint said, "but if someone *did* send those three men to kill him, we'd be telling them that they failed. No, I have a friend in Labyrinth, Texas, named Rick Hartman . . ."

"I remember you talking about him from way back."

"He can find out for us whether or not a rich man named Wagner—we'll have to get the first name—really did die recently."

"All right," Hammer said, "so we've got to do that, *and* take care of the sheriff."

"And hopefully by tomorrow, so we can leave," Clint said. "If this is on the level we want to make sure young Mr. Wagner gets to Sacramento in plenty of time to collect his inheritance."

"Yeah," Hammer said, "we've got five thousand good reasons."

They left the hotel and went to the telegraph office together. They decided that Clint had better deal with the sheriff, since Hammer hadn't really spoken to the man since they arrived in town. That meant that Clint had to send the telegram to Rick first, and then go over to the sheriff's office.

Hammer waited outside the telegraph office while Clint sent the telegram.

"I think you'd better go back to the hotel," Clint said when he joined Hammer outside again.

"Why?"

"Well," Clint said, "we know that three men tried to kill Wagner yesterday. At least, we *think* we know that, but let's just say for argument's sake that's what happened. Who's to say that there were *only* three men hired?"

"I see what you mean," Hammer said. "Somebody else might try to kill him, and then we're out five thousand dollars each. You're right, I'll go and sit on him while you talk to the sheriff."

"Ridge isn't going to take my word for it," Clint said, "so when Wagner wakes up we'll take him right over there, too. I'll just prime the pump and meet you back at the hotel."

"Got it," Hammer said, and this time they split up.

TWELVE

"So he's up and around?" Sheriff Ridge said. "This Jack Wagner?"

"Yes," Clint said, "at least, he was. Right now he's at the hotel catching some rest in a real bed."

"Really?" Ridge said. "And who's paying for the room, *and* for the doctor?"

"I am," Clint said.

"And you still claim that you're not friends?"

"He'll pay me back," Clint said.

"Sure," Ridge said. "Well, I better go talk to him."

"He'll clear me with you," Clint said. "When he does, I'll be leaving town."

Ridge stood up, met Clint's eyes boldly and said, "I don't think that would be a bad idea."

"You seem to have changed your tune since yesterday," Clint said.

"I've decided that my town would be better off without the famous Gunsmith in it."

"I couldn't agree more," Clint said. "Uh, you won't be able to talk to Jack Wagner, yet. We're hoping that some rest will bring back the rest of his memory."

Ridge stopped short and said, "What's still missing?"

Clint cursed himself. Part of what was still missing was what happened yesterday, but of course he didn't want Ridge to know *that*.

"Just some bits and pieces," Clint said.

"Tell me something," the sheriff said. "When you and Hammer leave, will this young fella be leaving with you?"

"Yes," Clint said. "Three men tried to kill him yesterday, Sheriff. He is understandably afraid to travel alone."

"Understandably," Ridge said. "All right, I'll talk to him later. If he clears you, I'll be happy to see you leave."

"Not as happy as I'll be *to* leave," Clint said.

"Then we'll both get what we want."

The two men faced each other for a long moment, and then Clint turned and left. When he got to the hotel Hammer was sitting in the lobby.

"Well?"

"He wants us to leave almost as bad as we want to leave," Clint said.

"I doubt that. Is he comin' over here to talk to him?" Hammer asked.

"Later," Clint said.

"Is he going to believe him?"

"I don't know," Clint said. "I guess that depends on how good a story we cook up."

"Then we better get to work on one."

"Let's see if the saloon is open," Clint said. "If we have to invent a story, it'll be easier to do over a beer."

● ● ●

Later, after Jack Wagner was awake, they took him to the saloon for a beer and gave him the story that he would be telling the sheriff.

"What do you think?" Clint asked. "Can you remember all that?"

"There's nothing wrong with my memory," Wagner snapped impatiently, and then sheepishly added, "*now*, I mean."

"I know what you mean," Clint said. "Let's just make sure you have it straight."

Wagner repeated the story back to them, and did it quite well. So well, in fact, that he might have been a *born* liar.

The story was a simple one. Wagner was riding along with his wagon when he was attacked. He tried to outrun the three attackers, and his wagon turned over. When he came to, Clint and Hammer were there, and the three men were dead.

"Why don't I just tell him that I killed them?" Wagner asked afterward.

"Would you really want to do that?" Clint asked. "Admit to killing three men?"

"I . . . don't know."

"Besides," Hammer said, "there was no sign of a gun for you to have used. I think the sheriff would have an even harder time swallowing *that* as a story."

"You may be right," Wagner said. "What should I do now? Wait for him to come looking for me?"

"No," Clint said, "I think you should go to his office and get it over with."

"Will you come with me?" Wagner asked.

"No," Clint said, "we'll wait here. When you're done come back. We still have a lot to talk about."

"A-all right," Wagner said, standing. He was obviously nervous about talking to the sheriff. Maybe it was only because he had to lie to the law. At least, Clint hoped that was the reason. There was still a possibility that the young man was pulling the wool over their eyes. Clint, however, depended very heavily on his judgment of people, and he didn't think that was the case.

"Here I go," Wagner said.

"Just do it," Hammer said, "don't think so much about it."

"Right," Wagner said. "I'll, uh, be back soon."

They watched him walk from the saloon, obviously unsure of himself.

"The sheriff better buy his story," Hammer said, "or we're likely to be here a while."

"I think he'll buy it," Clint said, "even if he doesn't believe it."

THIRTEEN

Clint and Hammer waited in the saloon for Wagner to return, the only two customers there in the early afternoon. In fact, some of the tables still had the chairs stacked on top of them, and the bartender was still in the process of getting the place ready to do business.

"Two more?" the bartender asked them.

"Sure," Clint said, "why not."

"Second one's on the house," the man said, and brought them two fresh mugs.

"Did you tell the desk clerk at the hotel we'd be over here, in case an answer to your telegram comes?" Hammer asked.

"I told him," Clint said. "If the reply comes in they'll bring it over here."

"Are we leaving tomorrow even if a reply *doesn't* come back?"

"In that case we'll have to rely on our own judgment," Clint said. "I don't think Wagner is lying about the inheritance."

"I hear a 'but' in there, somewhere."

"Well . . . I'm not quite convinced about the amnesia," Clint said.

"What? Now you tell me."

"Let me put that a different way," Clint said, hastily. "I think there may be something he's still not telling us."

"I get that feeling, too," Hammer said, "but the prospect of five thousand dollars will make me put up with almost anything."

"And he may open up to us somewhere along the way," Clint said. "The important thing is whether or not we believe his inheritance story. We *know* somebody tried to kill him yesterday. That much is obvious."

"Right."

"So then we're committed to this."

"Right," Hammer said, and then added, "unless something happens to uncommit us."

Sheriff Ridge studied the young man seated across the desk from him. Wagner had finished telling the story Clint and Hammer had given him, and was now nervously waiting to see if the sheriff believed it.

"Why are you so nervous?" Ridge asked Wagner.

"I'm, uh, not used to talking to the law."

"Any reason why not?"

"I don't know," Wagner said. "Do people *usually* have contact with the law?"

"No," Ridge said, "not usually."

Ridge stared at Wagner, and the young man started to fidget in his seat.

"Sheriff, is there something else?"

"I'm not sure I believe you, Mr. Wagner."

"Why not?"

"Oh, I don't know," Ridge said. "Maybe you're

just trying to cover up for Clint Adams."

"Why would I do that?" Wagner asked. "I never met the man before yesterday, when he and Hammer stopped to help me out."

"That's what you say," Ridge said, "and what they say."

"So why would we lie?"

"I don't know," Ridge said, "but a lot of people lie to the law."

"How can you believe what anyone says, then?" Wagner asked. "Excuse me for saying so, Sheriff, but I don't think I would have your job for anything."

"Yes," Ridge said, his eyes dropping downward for a moment, "sometimes I feel the same way." He looked up at Wagner then and said, "All right, Mr. Wagner."

Wagner waited, then said, "Uh, all right . . . what?"

"You can go."

"You believe me?"

"Not necessarily," Ridge said, "but you can go."

"Can I leave town?"

"Frankly," Ridge said, "I wish you would, you *and* Hammer *and* Clint Adams."

Wagner stood up, unsure of himself. He half expected the sheriff to change his mind, but as he moved to the door the man just sat quietly behind his desk, watching him. When he finally made it outside, the office door closed behind him, he breathed deeply and started for the saloon.

"Here he is," Clint said, as Wagner walked into the saloon.

Wagner came over and sat down with them.

"How did it go?" Hammer asked.

"He said we could leave."

"He believed you?" the black man asked.

"I don't think so," Wagner said, "but he said we could leave."

"Well," Hammer said, "that's good enough for me. First thing tomorrow morning?"

"First light," Clint agreed.

"Do I have a horse?" Wagner asked.

Clint and Hammer looked at each other. They had already paid for Wagner's doctor bill and put him up in the hotel. Now they were going to have to buy him a horse.

"You know something?" Hammer said. "We're gonna have to add some expenses to that five thousand dollar fee—otherwise we might end up spending all our money before we even get it."

"Don't worry," Wagner said, "I'll take care of your expenses, too—uh, like something to eat?"

"Hammer, why don't you take our new friend over to that café and get him some lunch?" Clint said.

"What are you gonna do?" Hammer asked.

"I'll arrange for a horse, and pick up some supplies for the trip to California," Clint said.

They left the saloon together, Hammer and Wagner going one way to the café while Clint went the other way, to the livery stable.

Across the street from the saloon a man stood in a doorway, watching the three men separate. He'd had a chance at the young man earlier, when he left the saloon alone to go to the sheriff's office, but the man decided not to make an attempt in town. He was going to wait until Wagner left town, even if he left with the other two men. It was just going to be their hard luck if they were with him.

That would mean that they'd never have the chance to learn to pick their friends more carefully.

FOURTEEN

That night Hammer once again got into a poker game at the saloon. Clint sat at a table with Jack Wagner, learning all he could learn about the young man. Honey kept coming over to ask if they needed anything.

"I have a brother and a sister," Wagner said, "both older. I get along better with my sister than I do with my brother. You see, my brother and I are opposites. He's always *wanted* to be involved in my father's business, but he hasn't got the brains. I *could* have worked with my father very easily, but I never wanted to."

"It would make your brother pretty angry if your father left you the business, wouldn't it?"

"I guess it would."

"Mad enough to have you killed?"

"My own brother?" Wagner asked, thinking it over. "I don't . . . think so."

"But you can't say for sure, can you?"

"No," he said. "Vic is pretty . . . ambitious, and like I said, we've never been that close. I suppose if it meant a fortune to him, and control of our father's business empire, he *might* not stop at killing me."

"But not your sister."

"No, Donna's different. Besides, my father would never leave his business to my sister. He'd never admit that a woman could run it."

"What about your mother?"

"My mother died years ago," Wagner said. "She was something special. I mean, maybe my father and I, and my brother and I never got along, but we *all* loved my mother. She was . . . special."

"So your father wasn't married when he died?"

"Oh, yes," Wagner said, "he was married to Lydia. What a bitch! Lydia is only about a year or two older than my sister, Donna. She's beautiful, but *cold*. Now I *could* see her having me killed with no problem."

"So it could be your brother, or your stepmother. Anyone else?"

Wagner thought it over and said, "There's no one else I can think of who would benefit from having me killed."

"No other employees of your father's? Lawyer? Accountant?"

"No, my father would never let control pass to someone who wasn't blood."

"Well then I guess it has to be your brother or your stepmother."

"I vote for my stepmother, then," Wagner said. "Then again, for all I know . . ." He trailed off, as if he'd been about to say something and now decided not to.

"What, Jack? Don't hold anything back from me. If I've got to keep you alive I've got to know all I can."

"Well . . . when I left home I know my brother was sleeping with my stepmother."

"I see," Clint said. "Do you think you father knew?"

"My father would probably kill them both if he knew," Wagner said, "but he'd do it himself."

"You almost sound proud of him," Clint said.

"Yeah," Wagner said, after a moment, "I guess I always was. I mean, I didn't approve of the way he did business, but what he accomplished was incredible. Yeah, I was proud of him."

Honey came over at that point and said, "Can I get you fellas another beer?" She was looking directly at Clint when she asked.

"Sure, Honey," Clint said, "two more."

As she walked away Wagner said to Clint, "I better get my own hotel room tonight, or I'm gonna be in the way. I can see that."

"Don't worry about it," Clint said. "We'll work something out."

"No, really—"

"I don't think I want to pay for a third hotel room, Jack," Clint said. "We'll work something out."

"Oh," Wagner said, "okay."

Honey brought the beers back, pressed her hip against Clint's shoulder as she put them down, then sashayed away, twitching her hips. Wagner watched her walk away, then felt as if he had to apologize to Clint.

"Sorry."

"For what? She walks like that so men *will* watch," Clint said. "She'd be upset if you didn't."

"What about you? I mean, aren't you two—"

"We're not engaged, Jack," Clint said, picking up

his beer. "Don't worry about it."

They sat in silence for a few moments and then Wagner said, "You know, I just thought of something."

"What?"

"If we get to a big enough town, with a big enough bank, I may be able to send to Sacramento for some money from my sister. You know, for expenses."

"That would help," Clint said, "but by the time that happens we might already be in California. Let's not count on it, but we'll keep it in mind."

FIFTEEN

At one point during the night the sheriff walked in, approached the bar and accepted a beer from the bartender. He drank it slowly, his back to the bar, his eyes roaming the room. Every so often his eyes would stop on Clint and Wagner. Clint was glad the man never walked over to them, though. He really had nothing left to say to the lawman, and he was relieved when the man finally finished his beer and left.

"I keep expecting him to change his mind and arrest me," Clint said.

"Or me," Wagner said.

"Jack, you still have no memory whatsoever of what happened yesterday?"

"Yesterday," Wagner said, "the day before, hell no, the last week is still a blank."

"Well," Clint said, scratching his cheek, "it occurs to me that you might actually be better off *not* remembering what happened."

"You mean it might be so bad I don't *want* to remember?" Wagner said.

"Maybe," Clint said, "and maybe when we get to

Sacramento you can get checked by another doctor who knows more about amnesia than this doctor did."

"My father's doctor," Wagner said, "would keep up on all new medical developments—if he's still alive, that is. He's older than my father."

"That's something we didn't discuss," Clint said, surprised at himself.

"What?"

"How did your father die?"

Wagner thought a moment, then stared across the table at Clint.

"You know," he said, "I've either forgotten, or I never knew." He thought about it some more and added, "I don't think my sister ever told me. I think the message just said that he was dead."

"He was dead?" Clint asked. "Or he had died?"

Jack Wagner thought again and then said, "Uh, I think the words were, 'he's dead.' Jesus, do you think *he* was killed?"

"I have no reason to think that, Jack," Clint said. "I was just asking, that's all. Maybe you'd better get back to the hotel and get some sleep."

"I am a little tired."

"Come on, I'll take you back."

"And then what? Will you be coming back here?"

"No," Clint said, "I'll bunk in with Hammer tonight. I'll take the floor."

"I hate taking your bed away from you," Wagner said. "Why not let me sleep on the floor in your room while you take the bed?"

"No," Clint said, "I want you to spend this last night in a bed. Who knows, a good night's sleep might help bring your memory back. Hammer and

I have shared a room before. There won't be a problem."

"Oh," Wagner said, "oh, well, okay, if it's not problem."

They got up and started across the room. Hammer saw them and nodded to Clint. From the stack of chips in front of him, Clint didn't think the black man would be quitting anytime soon.

Before he could get to the door he was intercepted by Honey.

"Should I come over after work?" she asked, keeping her voice down.

"I don't know, Honey," he said, and then explained that he'd given his room away to Wagner and would be sharing Hammer's for the night.

"That could get crowded," she said.

"I agree."

"Maybe when Hammer is finished he'll take his room back," she proposed, "and then you and I can go somewhere else."

"Like where?" Clint asked.

"Well," she said, "I do have a room, too, you know—*with* a bed."

"Well," Clint said, "why don't we wait till the time comes and see what happens?"

"I never just wait and see what happens, Clint," she said. "I make what *I* want to happen happen. I'll talk to Hammer, and to Michelle and Alice—and I will see *you* later."

He watched her glide away from him, playing the room, and then turned and stepped outside with Wagner.

"I am getting in the way, aren't I, Clint?" Wagner asked.

"For five thousand dollars," Clint said to him, "you can get in my way anytime. Come on . . ."

Then they started across the street to the hotel. Neither of them saw the man who was watching them from a darkened doorway across the street.

SIXTEEN

It actually worked out to everyone's advantage.

Clint was awake when Hammer finally returned to his room, and he wasn't alone. He walked in with Michelle on one arm and Alice on the other.

"Hammer," Clint said as his friend turned the light up on the lamp.

"Clint, my friend," Hammer said. "I brought some company."

"Not for me," Clint said.

"No," Hammer said, "for me, and for our friend next door."

"What?"

"Alice, here, is going to go next door and keep young Wagner company. Ain't that right, Alice?"

"Whatever you say, honey," Alice said. She was the willowy brunette with the brutally sexy mouth.

"What do you think?" Hammer asked Clint. "Will she shock his memory back?"

Clint sat up on the floor and said, "You know? That might work."

"Oh, yeah," Hammer said, "I forgot. I brought some company for you, too."

"Hammer—"

"She's waiting downstairs."

Honey, he thought. Well, why not? Hammer would be here in the next room, and Alice would be in the room with him.

"All right, then," Clint said, getting to his feet, "you can have your room to yourself."

"Thank you," Hammer said. "Uh, would you let Alice into Wagner's room on your way past."

"Sure," Clint said. "Come on, Alice."

Alice released Hammer's arm and linked her arm in Clint's.

"Of course," she said to him in the hall, giving him the full effect of that lovely mouth, "you and I could both go down and see Honey—"

"I don't think so, Alice," he said.

"Don't like to share and be shared, huh?"

"Afraid not."

"Well," she said, smiling at him, "maybe another time, huh?"

"Maybe," he said. He unlocked the door to the other room and swung it open. The lamp was dimly lit and he could see Wagner as he sat up in bed.

"Wha—"

"Brought you some company, kid," Clint said, letting Alice into the room.

"Hi," she said brightly, and Clint closed the door on them.

As he went downstairs he sincerely hoped that Jack Wagner remembered how to do *that*.

In the lobby he found Honey waiting, a shawl covering her bare shoulders and cleavage.

"You're leaving tomorrow, aren't you?" she asked as they left the hotel.

"I'm afraid so."

"Well," she said, putting her head against his arm, "we have tonight to say good-bye, don't we?"

"That we do."

The man standing across the street suddenly realized that he had a chance to cut the odds down. He didn't have to kill this man, just disable him so he couldn't travel with Wagner.

As the man and the woman started down the street the man stepped from his doorway and started following them.

SEVENTEEN

"Honey."

"Yes?"

"Are we coming to an alley ahead anywhere?"

"Why?" she asked, giggling. "Can't you wait?"

"Just answer me."

"Yes," she said, "another block and there'll be an alley on the right. Why?"

"I'm going to step off into that alley. When I do I want you to keep walking."

"Why?"

"Because somebody is following us," Clint said, "and I want to find out who it is."

"Following us? Why?"

"Don't ask any more questions," he said, as he spotted the mouth of the alley, "just keep walking."

As they came to the mouth of the alley he stepped into it quickly, hoping that the man following them was not close enough to notice.

He waited, back pressed against the wall of the building, and when the man came into view he reached out, grabbed him and pulled him into the alley.

"Hey!" the man said, trying to regain his balance.

"Why are you following me?" Clint demanded.

"What the hell are you talking about?" the man demanded.

The alley was dark, and Clint could make out the silhouette of the man, but couldn't see his face very well. He was a tall man, wide in the shoulders, and he sounded fairly young.

"Are you crazy?" the man demanded. "How would you like me to start shouting for the law?"

"Go ahead," Clint said. "Then you can explain to the sheriff why you're following me."

"I ain't following anybody," the man said. "I don't know what you're talking about. I'm getting out of here, pal."

The man started moving toward the mouth of the alley and for a moment Clint was undecided about what to do. *Was* the man following him, or was he just jumping at shadows now that he and Hammer had a job?

"Wait a minute—" Clint said, but at that moment Honey came back and stepped into the alley.

"What's going on—"

"Honey," Clint said, "move!" but he was too late. The man moved quickly, grabbing Honey and placing her between himself and Clint.

"It's dark, friend," the man said, "but believe me, I've got a gun pressed to the lady's back, don't I, miss? Tell him!"

"Yes, he does!" Honey blurted.

"Okay," Clint said, "so now what?"

"Now nothing," the man said. "I made a mistake. I'm gonna back out of here and be on my way. Don't follow or I'll kill the woman."

"No good, friend," Clint said. "You're not taking her with you."

"I'll kill her!"

"And then I'll kill you."

There was a moment of silence and then the man said, "What do you suggest?"

"Leave her," Clint said, "and I won't follow."

Another moment and then the man asked, "I have your word?"

"You have my word," Clint said.

"All right," the man said.

"Just remember this," Clint said. "If I see you again you won't get off this easy."

"Yeah," the man said, "sure."

Abruptly he pushed Honey at Clint and started running. Clint moved and caught Honey before she could fall to the ground.

"Are you all right?" he asked, setting her back on her feet.

"Yes," she said, "I'm fine—but aren't you going after him?"

"No," he said, "I gave him my word."

"What now?" she asked.

"Well," he said, "I'm still in favor of what we were planning to do."

"But—w-what about that man?"

"What about him?" Clint said. "I don't know what he wanted, but I know he won't try it again tonight."

"Aren't you curious?"

"Sure I am," he said, "but I have a feeling that I'll be seeing him again soon. I'll find out then what he wanted."

"He'll come after you even after what you told him?" she asked. "Won't he be too frightened?"

"I don't think he knew who I was when he started following us," Clint said, "and I sure didn't tell him. No, he'll try again—but not for a while. Come on," he said, taking her arm, "you were going to show me where your room is."

She clung to his arm tightly as they walked the rest of the way to her room.

Clint had decided that it would do no good to tell Hammer and Jack Wagner about the man who had followed him the night before. He'd tell Hammer eventually, but not in front of Wagner. There was no point in causing the younger man any more concern.

Clint met Hammer and Wagner at the hotel. Hammer had already collected Clint's gear from his room and had checked them out. When he saw Clint enter the hotel he smiled broadly.

"Glad you could make it," Hammer said, handing Clint his saddlebags.

"Just about," Clint said. "I can hardly walk."

"Me neither," Hammer said. "That Michelle has a special way of saying good-bye to a fella."

"So does Honey."

Hammer looked at Wagner, who had been quiet the whole time, and said, "How about you, kid? Did you do all right last night?"

"A gentleman never tells," Wagner said, and started for the livery stable.

"Well, that's something," Clint said.

"What?" Hammer asked.

Clint looked at Hammer and said, "He remembered that he's a gentleman."

EIGHTEEN

The first day of travel went uneventfully, and that night when they camped Clint told Wagner to collect wood for the fire. While the young man was doing that he and Hammer saw to the horses. That was when Clint told Hammer about the man who had followed him in town.

"You know," Hammer said, "the whole time we were in town I had the feeling I was being watched."

"Why didn't you say anything about it?"

Hammer grinned and said, "I thought I was being watched by women."

"Well, maybe you were being watched by the same man who was following me," Clint said, thoughtfully, "and maybe by someone else—which would mean that we have *two* people to worry about."

"At least," Hammer said. "If what Jack has told us is true, there's enough money in this for his brother or stepmother to hire a dozen guns."

"That's a cheery thought," Clint said.

"I'd still like to know who killed those other three men," Hammer said. "If it was Jack himself at least we'd know that he can handle a gun."

"Maybe we should find out if he *can* handle one," Clint said.

"Handle one what?" Wagner said. He had returned with an armload of wood for the fire.

"A gun," Hammer said, taking the wood from him. "Can you handle a gun?"

"What do you mean by 'handle'?" Wagner asked. "I can *fire* a gun."

"Can you hit what you shoot at?" Clint asked.

"You mean like a man?"

"Like a man," Hammer said.

"I don't know," Wagner said, "I've never fired a gun at a man."

"What have you fired a gun at?" Hammer asked.

"A target," Wagner said, "an animal."

"Did you hit it?" Hammer asked as he started the fire.

"What? The target, or the animal?"

"Either one."

"No."

"Come close?"

"No."

"You remember this, Jack?" Clint asked. "I mean, it couldn't be that you *can* shoot but have forgotten that fact?"

Wagner thought a moment and then said, "If I *have* forgotten it, I wouldn't be able to *say* that I forgot it, would I?"

Clint looked at Hammer, who said, "Don't look at me. If I tried to understand that I'd end up with a helluva headache."

"Maybe we should just test him out," Clint said. "Hammer, give him your gun."

Hammer stood up, took his gun from his holster

and handed it to Wagner. Clint looked around for a likely target, then pointed to a large deadwood tree about twenty feet away.

"Try that," he said.

"Which branch?" Wagner asked.

"Just hit the tree, Jack," Hammer said, "we'll worry about branches later."

Wagner shrugged, raised the gun and fired. The bullet kicked up dirt about three feet in front of the tree. Hammer looked at Clint.

"Get my gun back before he ruins it," he said.

"Take it easy," Clint said. "Come on, Jack, let's move a little closer."

Clint and Wagner walked until they were about ten feet from the tree.

"Okay," Clint said, "try it now."

Wagner raised the gun and fired, all in one motion—and missed.

"Try it slower," Clint said. "Raise the gun, aim at the tree, and then fire."

"Okay."

Wagner raised the gun, closed one eye and jerked the trigger—and missed.

"Okay," Clint said, "try this. Point the gun like it was your finger, and just *squeeze* the trigger instead of jerking it."

Wagner nodded, then raised the gun, pointed it and squeezed the trigger. The bullet nicked the tree, stripping just a piece of bark from it.

"Hey," Hammer said, "he's a natural."

Clint took the gun from Wagner and said, "Let's try a rifle."

He handed Hammer his rifle and fetched the Winchester he was carrying these days. He handed it to

Wagner, who held it in both hands, studying it.

"Try that."

"From here?" Wagner asked.

"From right here."

Wagner put the rifle to his shoulder, sighted down the barrel, and fired. He hit the tree dead center.

"Let's back up," Clint said.

They moved back to the original twenty-foot distance, and Wagner fired again—and hit the tree dead center.

Clint looked at Hammer who said, "Whoa."

"Let's move back farther," Clint said.

"Okay."

At fifty feet Clint said, "Stop."

Wagner raised the rifle, sighted, and fired—and missed.

"Jesus," Hammer said, "I was starting to worry."

"Sorry," Wagner said, "I guess I'm just not very good with a gun."

"That's all right," Clint said, taking the rifle back. "We just wanted to know."

Clint ejected the spent shells and replaced them with live rounds, and then put the rifle down near his saddle.

"What about cooking?" he asked Wagner. "Can you cook?"

"I think so."

"Good," Clint said, "then rustle something up."

Wagner put a pot of coffee on the fire then prepared some bacon and beans, with enough grease to soften the hard chunks of bread they had brought along.

"What'd you do to these beans?" Hammer asked.

"Why?" Wagner asked.

"They're delicious," Hammer said. "When I make them they just sort of . . . lie there."

"It's just something I do with the beans and bacon," Wagner said. "Something nobody else does."

"Well, keep doin' it," Hammer said. He looked at Clint and added, "If he can't shoot, at least he can cook."

"Who said I can't shoot?" Wagner said. "I hit the tree with the rifle, didn't I?"

"That's right," Hammer said, looking at Clint, "we're safe as long as he only has to shoot at a tree from twenty feet or less."

Clint ignored the comment, put down his empty plate and poured himself another cup of coffee.

"Let's set the watches," Clint said. "I'll go first, then Jack, and then you, Hammer."

"Fine with me," Hammer said, "I'm an early riser, anyway."

"Sure," Clint said, "on the trail, where there are no women."

Hammer grinned and said, "Ain't nothin' else to do but get up early and get moving."

"I'll clean up," Wagner said.

"Hey, Jack," Hammer said, "if you don't mind, you can do all the cookin' between here and California."

"I don't mind, Hammer," Wagner said. "In fact, I like cooking."

"Good," Hammer said, "then it's settled?"

"Far as I'm concerned," Wagner said.

"Fine with me," Clint said.

Wagner made sure there was a full pot of coffee on the fire for Clint's watch, and then turned in.

Hammer had one more cup of coffee with Clint before turning in.

"Why do I get the feeling there's more than a week he can't remember," Hammer said.

"I know," Clint said, looking over his shoulder at Wagner. The young man had wrapped himself in a blanket and had his back to them.

"He couldn't remember that he can't *shoot* and that he *can* cook," Clint said. "That goes back more than just a week."

"I wonder what else he can't remember," Hammer said, pouring the remnants of his coffee into the fire.

"Or what he *can* remember," Clint said, "and isn't telling us."

NINETEEN

Clint woke Wagner for his watch, and the younger man asked Clint to sit with him for a few minutes. Wagner poured them both a cup of coffee.

"What is it?"

"I'm beginning to realize that there are more gaps in my memory than I . . . remember," Wagner said.

"Like what?"

"Well . . . I couldn't remember whether or not I can shoot a gun, and I *thought* I could cook, but I couldn't *remember* whether I could or not."

Clint looked at the younger man, the confused look on his face, the bandage on his head. Was he being truthful, or had he heard what Clint and Hammer were talking about a few hours ago? Was he just covering his tracks?

"It must be rough," Clint said.

"Believe me," Wagner said, his eyes widening, "it's no picnic. Jesus . . ."

"What?"

Wagner looked at him with an incredibly sad look and said, "I can't remember if I've ever been on a picnic."

Looking into the young man's face Clint was once again acutely aware of the fact that he *wanted* to believe him—he *did* believe him . . . almost. The cynic in him just wouldn't let him *totally* believe him.

"How can I remember my mother, my father, my relatives . . . I can remember a lot about my past life in Sacramento . . . even my childhood . . . but I can't remember other things, like whether I can shoot, or cook . . ." He looked at Clint suddenly and said, "Do you know that last night, when Alice came into the hotel room, I was *scared*. I didn't remember if I'd ever been with a woman before."

"And what happened?"

"It just sort of . . . came to me," he said. "I mean, I *knew* what to do without remembering if I'd ever done it before."

"She didn't complain, did she?"

"Well, no . . . but still, it was the strangest thing . . . I just can't get used to this, Clint . . . this not *knowing* . . ."

"I don't know what to tell you, Jack," Clint said. "Maybe when you get home it'll all come back. Maybe it'll *never* come back, totally. Either way you're going to have to be able to deal with it, and go on with your life."

"I know, I know . . ."

"Of course, on the other hand," Clint said, "soon you'll be rich enough to have the best doctors in the world examine you. Maybe they can help you."

Wagner rubbed his jaw and said thoughtfully, "I guess you're right. All I've got to do is get there in one piece, right?"

Clint clapped the younger man on the shoulder

and said, "Hammer and I will get you there in one piece, Jack."

"Really?"

"All you have to do is what you're told," Clint said, "and we'll make it."

Clint stood up and looked down at him.

"What's it like, Clint?" Wagner asked.

"What?"

"To be as confident as you and Hammer are?" Wagner said. "To know that you can handle anything that comes along?"

Clint grinned at the younger man and said, "You mean you don't remember?"

Wagner smiled grimly at the joke and said, "Oh, I don't think I *ever* knew that. As much as I *can* remember, I was never very confident. Is it something you can learn?"

Clint thought a moment and said, "I don't know if it's something you can learn, Jack. It's certainly something you *feel*." Clint shook his head and said, "I don't know, maybe it's something you can *learn* to *feel*."

"Well, I wish I could learn it."

Clint touched the younger man's shoulder again, reassuringly, then walked to his saddle to collect his rifle. He walked back to the fire and handed it to Wagner, who accepted it, tentatively.

"If you have to warn us," he instructed Jack, "fire a shot."

"Warn you about what?" Wagner asked, suddenly looking *and* sounding alarmed.

"About anything," Clint said. "You're on watch, Jack. If you hear something, or see something, wake me up. If something happens and you have to wake us up fast, fire a shot."

"Oh," Wagner said, "O-okay."

"Nothing may happen, Jack," Clint said, "but you have to be ready for anything."

"All right," Wagner said. "I understand, Clint."

"You going to be all right?"

"Sure," Wagner said, "sure, I can do this, Clint. Don't worry."

"All right," Clint said. "Wake Hammer in a few hours, okay?"

"Okay."

Clint went over to his blanket and lay down on it, using his saddle as a pillow. He wondered if he should stay awake a while, then decided to leave Jack Wagner on his own. It might go a long way toward helping him become self-confident.

TWENTY

Clint woke the next morning on his own and joined Hammer at the fire.

"I guess the kid did okay on watch, huh?" he asked, pouring himself a cup of coffee.

"He did fine," Hammer said. "What do you think he's gonna do when he gets to Sacramento? I mean, if he inherits his father's company."

Clint shrugged and said, "I don't know. From what he says he sure won't be able to run it the way his old man did. He'll probably have enough money to hire someone to run it for him."

"Or maybe he could sell it and make even *more* money," Hammer said.

"Could be."

"I was thinkin', though," Hammer said.

"About what?"

He turned and looked over at Wagner, who was still asleep.

"Well, we don't know how much the kid is supposed to collect," Hammer said. "After all, he *did* leave home. What if he doesn't get enough to pay us?"

"I guess we'll just have to deal with that when the time comes," Clint said. "We could always take it out of his hide, right?"

"Good point," Hammer said.

"I'll wake him," Clint said. "We want to get an early start."

"I'll saddle the horses," Hammer said, "you clean up here."

"Right."

Clint walked over to the sleeping Jack Wagner and nudged him with his foot. The young man came awake slowly, staring up at Clint with gummed eyes.

"What—"

"Time to get started, Jack," Clint said.

"Uh, okay," Wagner said, and closed his eyes again.

Clint shook his head and bent over to shake Wagner again . . . and the move saved his life. He heard the bullet whiz over his head even before he heard the shot.

"What?" Wagner shouted, coming awake. He sat up straight and slammed his head into Clint's. He just missed reopening his wound, but the clash of heads staggered Clint, who went back a couple of steps and then fell.

Hammer, hearing the shot and seeing Clint fall, thought that his friend was hit.

"Clint!"

As he rushed to Clint's side there was another shot and dirt kicked up about a foot from where Jack Wagner was sitting on the ground. He was still not fully awake, and now his head hurt from the impact with Clint's head.

"Move! Move!" Hammer shouted at him. He bent over Clint and shouted, "Are you hit?"

There was some blood on Clint's head where the skin had split when he made contact with Wagner's head.

"I'm fine," he said to Hammer.

"Your head," Hammer said. "Ain't you hit?"

"No, I'm not hit!" Clint snapped back.

There was a third shot and Hammer felt the impact on his right foot.

"Shit!" he said.

"Move!" Clint said. He put his hands against Hammer's chest and *pushed* the man away from him. For Wagner's benefit Clint shouted, "Take cover, dammit!"

All three of them were scrambling now, trying to find some sort of cover as shots began to rain down on them from . . . somewhere.

The only cover that was available was their own saddles, and they were all lying on the ground behind them now.

"Jesus, where's it coming from?" Hammer said.

"Above," Clint said, "the shots have to be coming from above us, so that means that ridge over there."

He pointed directly behind them. They had come over the ridge the previous night before making camp.

"How many you figure?" Hammer asked.

"At least two shooters," Clint said, "maybe more."

"How do you figure it?"

"I don't know," Clint said. "The first shot was at me. That could mean one of two things."

"One," Hammer said, "it's somebody out to collect your reputation."

"And two," Clint said, "they were just trying to get rid of me first before going after you and Wagner. Hammer, are you hit?"

"A bullet took off the heel of my right boot," Hammer said. "That's *too* close. What about you? Your head's bleeding."

Clint touched his forehead and looked at the blood on his finger.

"I banged heads with the kid."

"Kid, you okay?" Hammer asked, looking behind him.

"What's happening?" Wagner demanded. He was finally awake.

"Kid," Hammer said, "if you wanna survive out here you're gonna have to learn to wake up a lot faster than that."

"Who's shooting at us?" Wagner asked.

"We don't know that, yet," Hammer said. He looked at Clint and asked, "How we gonna find out?"

"I don't know," Clint said, keeping his eye on the ridge, "maybe they'll let us know."

The sun was coming up from behind them, shining on the ridge, and now he saw the reflection of light from someone's rifle. One flash, then a second, and *maybe* a third.

"Two shooters," he said, "maybe three."

"We have to make a move," Hammer said. "We're too easy down here."

"Maybe," Clint said, "and maybe we should wait for *them* to make a move."

"They have better cover than we do," Hammer said.

"What about the horses?" Clint asked.

Hammer looked over to where the animals were picketed—each of their saddle horses and one pack animal—and they were still there and still secured, although three of them were skittish. Duke, Clint's big black gelding, was standing stock still, calm as could be.

"Somebody's got to watch the horses," Clint said. "If they get to them, we're as good as finished."

"I'll watch them," Hammer said. "Cover me."

"Wait, wait," Clint said, "before you go we have to know what we're gonna do."

"Well, hell," Hammer said, "if *I'm* gonna watch the horses, then *you're* gonna have to make some kind of a move on them."

"Why me?"

"Hey," Hammer said, "you're the man with the big rep."

TWENTY-ONE

Clint grabbed his rifle and said, "Hey, kid."

"What?" Wagner said.

"Here."

Clint passed the rifle over to him.

"What am I supposed to do with this?" Wagner asked. "They're more than twenty feet away!"

"I know that," Clint said.

"I don't—I can't even *see* them."

"Sure you can," Clint said. "Look up at the ridge."

"I *see* the ridge," Wagner said, "but I can't see where *they* are!"

"See those flashes of light?"

"What flashes—"

"Look up there, don't look at me!" Clint snapped. "Keep watching. See it? That flash?"

"I saw it."

"That's one of them," Clint said. "That's the sun reflecting off someone's gun barrel. Keep watching, Jack . . . there, to the left. Another flash of light. Did you see it?"

"I saw it."

"And there might be another one farther to the

left," Clint explained. "If there is, he's smarter than the other two because he's not letting the sun reflect off his weapon."

"All right," Wagner said, "all right . . . so what am I supposed to do now?"

Clint wished he had Hammer here for this, but they needed someone reliable to keep an eye on the horses. He was going to *have* to use this kid for covering fire.

"I'm going up that ridge, Jack," Clint said, "and you're going to cover me."

"They'll kill you."

"Maybe," Clint said. "You're going to help me get there, though."

"How?"

"By firing that rifle as fast as you can."

"But . . . but I can't *hit* anything, Clint," Wagner complained.

"*They* don't know that," Clint said, "and by the time they realize it, maybe I'll be close enough to do some damage. Just make a lot of noise and fire in their direction. Who knows? You might get lucky and actually hit something."

"That *would* be lucky," Wagner said.

"Okay, now keep quiet a give me a minute to think this over."

If Clint was going to run for the ridge and start up, he needed someplace along the way to stop for cover. His eyes covered the space between them and the shooters and he finally picked out his spot. About a third of the way up there was a depression. It wasn't much in the way of cover, but it was better than nothing. At least they wouldn't have a totally clear shot at him. In fact, they might even have to stand to fire at him, and that was all he needed.

Before starting he dug into his saddlebag and came up with the little Colt New Line that he used occasionally as a belly gun. It didn't have much range, but it would make him feel better to have the extra fire power available, if he needed it.

"Okay, kid," Clint said, "when I tell you, start shooting."

"You're going to get killed," Wagner said, "and it's going to be my fault."

"I'm not going to get killed, kid," Clint said. "I've led a pretty charmed life up to now, and I'm not ready to cash in my chips yet. Just get ready."

"I'm ready."

Wagner raised the rifle and waited.

"Now!" Clint shouted, and started running.

Wagner began to fire, letting shots go as quickly as he could work the action on the rifle.

Clint started running, hoping that it *wasn't* time for him to cash out.

TWENTY-TWO

On the ridge Sam Kelly snapped, "Goddammit, I told you *not* to let the sun reflect off your guns."

"How we supposed to do that?" Del Leonard complained.

"Keep the rifles down until you see something you can fire at," Kelly said.

Sam Kelly was the man who had been following Clint Adams back in Taylor. He was *still* angry that he had let himself be taken by Adams, but then he only found out who he was dealing with after that incident—and *then* only by accident. He had heard two men talking and one of them mentioned that the Gunsmith was in town. It was then that Kelly realized that was who the man had to be. He had immediately telegraphed Sacramento to tell his employers that number one he needed more money to hire more help and number two, he needed more money to go up against the Gunsmith.

He had waited in Taylor while all the monetary transactions had been taken care of. Only after he had gotten a telegraph message from one of his men that the money was in his bank did he start after

Adams, Wagner, and the black man.

He had hired two men, Del Leonard and Tom Bonner, who he had found in Taylor, to go after them with him. They were drifters who'd do just about anything for money, killing included. Unfortunately, he could tell that they weren't very good at it. Still, he had already lost three men who worked for him—shit, he *still* didn't know exactly what had happened to them—and he needed to hire new help fast. If Adams and the kid got away from him this time, they'd probably have to be dealt with in Sacramento. If that happened, he was going to owe somebody their money back, and he didn't like that idea.

"What are we gonna do now?" Bonner asked. "Why don't we go down there and get them?"

"You want to do that?" Kelly asked. "Be my guest, go ahead. We'll cover you from here."

Bonner looked at Kelly, then bit his lip and shook his head.

"Never mind," he said, "you're ramrodding this thing. I'll wait for you to decide what to do."

"Good man," Kelly said. At least this one knew how to listen.

"What about their horses?" Leonard asked. "If we can separate them from their horses they'll be all ours."

"I thought of that," Kelly said, "but they'd have the animals covered by now."

"What about—"

"Shut up and let me think," Kelly said.

He couldn't believe his luck. He'd had Clint Adams right in his sights and the man had to bend over just at the last moment. Jesus, he almost *had*

the Gunsmith! What a feather in his cap that would
have been.

"What the hell—" Del Leonard said.

"What—" Kelly started to ask, but then someone
started firing from down below.

"Who's that?" Bonner asked.

Kelly looked and saw that Clint Adams was on
his feet and running toward them.

"He's crazy," Bonner said.

"Keep down!" Leonard shouted.

It only took a moment for Kelly to realize that
whoever was laying down the cover fire was doing
a lousy job of it. He was making noise, but wasn't
coming close to *hitting* anything.

"He's fuckin' crazy!" Bonner said again.

"Shoot him!" Kelly said.

"But the coverin' fire—" Leonard started, but Kelly
cut him off viciously.

"There *is* no covering fire, dammit," Kelly shouted,
but he had no time to explain it to them.

He stood then and sighted down his rifle barrel.
Adams was running and moving from side to side.
He tried to lead him and fired and thought he hit
the man, but he kept coming. Before he could fire
again, though, the Gunsmith had fallen into some
sort of a depression in the ground about a third of
the way up the ridge. He just couldn't see him,
dammit.

"Where is he?" Bonner asked, standing up, looking for the man with the barrel of his rifle.

"Get back down!" Kelly said, dropping back down
himself.

At that moment he saw the Gunsmith come into
view and fire one shot. He heard the bullet smack

wetly into Tom Bonner's chest. The man fell backward and stared sightlessly at the early morning sky.

"Jesus," Del Leonard said, staring down at his dead friend.

"Fuck," Sam Kelly said.

Clint Adams ducked back down, ejected the empty shell, inserted a live one in its place and said to himself, "One down."

TWENTY-THREE

Clint put his hand up to his shoulder and it came away bloody. He probed the wound and found that the bullet had dug a furrow in passing. It was a clean wound and would heal. He didn't have to worry about it. His luck was still holding.

He knew he had hit the man dead center in the chest. If he wasn't dead, he was mortally wounded. There was definitely one down, and possibly two more to go.

He couldn't be seen from above, but from below he knew he was visible to both Hammer and Jack Wagner. He waved to let them know he was all right, then tried to tell Wagner by the use of sign language to get ready to fire again. He was going up the hill this time—all the way up.

He hoped the man understood.

"What's he saying?" Wagner shouted. "He's just waving his arms."

Hammer could hear Wagner from where he stood with the horses, and he could see Clint. He made a decision right then. He decided that whoever the men on the ridge were, they weren't after the horses now. They'd be too concerned with Clint. Hammer left the horses and moved back to Jack Wagner's side.

"He's gonna keep going," Hammer said. "He'll need more coverin' fire."

"Are you going to shoot?" Wagner asked.

"Yeah," Hammer said, "but so are you. The more noise we make the better off he'll be. Get ready."

"I'm ready."

"So am I," Hammer said. "Go ahead, Clint, make your move . . ."

Clint saw that Hammer had joined Wagner and knew that his covering fire would now be more effective. That bolstered his confidence.

He turned and peered up at the top of the ridge. He couldn't see anyone, but he knew they'd still be there. These men would be getting paid for a job, and they wouldn't give it up that easily.

He took a deep breath, then stood up and started running again.

From behind him he heard Hammer and Wagner start to fire.

From above Kelly and Leonard saw Clint Adams running up the hill.

Kelly knew immediately that *this* time—for some reason—the fire from below was more accurate.

Unfortunately, Del Leonard didn't realize that.

"I got 'im, I got 'im!" he shouted, standing up.

"Leonard, get down, dammit!" Kelly shouted, but it was too late.

A rifle shot from down below struck Leonard in the shoulder, spinning him around. Kelly saw Adams

take advantage of that to fire his own gun, and that
shot hit Leonard squarely in the back. The man fell
over on top of his dead comrade. Kelly looked down
at the two dead men and saw them only as money
wasted.

He looked down the ridge and saw Adams still
coming, but the slope steepened here and the man
wasn't moving as well as he had been earlier.

This was his chance. The covering fire from below
had stopped. If he stood, and took one well-aimed
shot, it would take a lucky shot from down below
to stop him. He had a chance now to kill the Gunsmith, and he was going to take it.

He stood, and sighted down on the Gunsmith.

Clint felt the slope steepen and suddenly he felt as
if he were trying to run through molasses. He would
have been all right, though, if he hadn't stepped in a
hole right at that moment. He felt his foot go into a
chick hole and saw the man at the top of the ridge
stand up and aim his rifle. He was too far off balance
himself to do anything about it. It looked to him like
his luck had finally run out . . .

Hammer saw the man stand and sight down his
barrel at Clint, who seemed to have staggered.

"Shit!" he said, and stood up.

Jack Wagner also stood, and at the same moment
both men fired.

Just as Sam Kelly squeezed the trigger of his rifle
he felt the bullet smack into his chest.

A lucky shot, dammit, he thought as he fell over
backward . . .

• • •

Clint Adams felt the bullet strike him and he fell backward. In falling, he twisted his ankle, which was still stuck in the hole.

He didn't know what hurt more.

Hammer reached Clint and said, "Are you all right?"

"Get my foot out of this damned hole!" Clint snapped.

Hammer helped him get his foot free and then inspected him for damage. There was a bloody furrow on his right shoulder, and the last shot had hit him in the left arm. His ankle was surely injured, but none of these injuries looked life threatening.

"Your luck's holding," Hammer said, trying his bandanna around the wound in Clint's arm.

"Luck, hell," Clint said. "That fella had me dead to rights. That was a fine shot, Hammer."

"It sure was," the black man said.

"You're so modest," Clint said through tightly set teeth as Hammer pulled the bandanna tight.

Hammer looked Clint right in the eye and said, "What the hell do I have to be modest about? *I* missed."

TWENTY-FOUR

Clint insisted that he was all right to travel, once Hammer had bandaged the wound on his arm, and cleaned the one on his shoulder. His ankle was tender, but had not swelled, and besides—he said—they weren't going to be doing a lot of walking, were they?

Before they left, though, Hammer went up to the top of the ridge with Wagner to look at the bodies.

"From Clint's description," Hammer said, nudging Sam Kelly with the toe of his boot, "this could be the fella who followed him in town."

"What do you mean, followed him?"

Hammer realized that they hadn't let Wagner *know* that Clint had been followed, so he told him now.

"Why didn't you tell me before?" Wagner asked.

"Hell," Hammer said, "he didn't even tell *me* until after we left town. After that there didn't seem to be any point in telling you. Do you know this fella?"

"Never saw him before."

"And the other two?"

"Nope."

"That's all right," Hammer said, "they're probably just hired help. Go through their pockets, anyway."

"Their . . . pockets?" Wagner said.

"Go on," Hammer said, "they're dead, they won't help you."

While Wagner gingerly went through the pockets of the other two men Hammer gave the first man a thorough going over. He eventually found a telegraph message from a town in Texas, telling the man that fifteen thousand dollars *more* had been deposited in his bank account. Hammer whistled.

"What is it?" Wagner asked.

"This fella got paid a lot of money," Hammer said.

"By who?"

"That it doesn't say," Hammer said, tucking the telegraph message away in his pocket. He looked at Wagner and said, "His name was Sam Kelly. That mean anything to you?"

"No, nothing."

"You find anything on them?"

"Not much," Wagner said. "They each have over a hundred dollars, though."

"That means they were each *paid* a hundred dollars," Hammer said. "Keep it, we'll probably need it along the way."

"Isn't that robbing the dead?" Wagner asked.

"Kid," Hammer said, patiently, "they were *paid* that money to kill you—and us. I think we're entitled to it, don't you?"

"I suppose."

"Come on, let's go," Hammer said, looking

around. "We don't know if these fellas have any help comin'."

"I hope they don't," Wagner said.

"This makes two attempts on you, kid," Hammer said. "Somebody is sparing no expense. Let's keep it movin'."

They went back down to where they had left Clint. The horses were saddled and Hammer helped Clint climb up on Duke's back. As they rode away from camp he told Clint what he and Wagner had found.

"Fifteen thousand dollars *more*?" Clint said.

"That's right."

"I wonder how much he was paid in the first place," Clint said.

"I don't know," Hammer said, "but think why he might have asked for more."

"Because he lost three men?"

"What else?" Hammer asked.

"Because the kid has two bodyguards now?"

"Close," Hammer said. "Keep guessin'."

Clint frowned and said, "I hate guessing games, Hammer. Spell it out for me."

"Fifteen thousand to take care of two bodyguards, that's a lot," Hammer said. "I'd be flattered if someone thought I was worth that much, but I don't think I need to be flattered."

"I see where you're heading with this," Clint said, suddenly.

"*I* don't," Wagner said.

Hammer looked at Wagner and said, "The Gunsmith is worth fifteen thousand dollars, easy."

"The Gunsmith," Wagner said, frowning.

"Do you remember that name?" Hammer asked.

"Yes," the young man said, "I do."

"Well, that's who Clint is," Hammer said, and then before Clint could correct him he hastily added, "At least, that's what some folks call him."

"I didn't know that when I . . . when I hired you," Wagner said. "Should I have offered you more money?"

Hammer started to answer and Clint jumped in and said, "You offered plenty, Jack."

Hammer frowned and said to Clint, "You might want to reconsider that."

"Why?"

"Well, if this Sam Kelly knew who he was dealing with," Hammer said, "by now they know in Sacramento, too."

"What do you mean?" Wagner asked.

Hammer looked at him and said, "Kid, by the time we get to Sacramento they're gonna be ready for us—they're gonna be ready for Clint Adams."

"Oh," Wagner said, "well . . . will we be ready for them?"

"Kid," Hammer said, exchanging a glance with Clint, "we're *always* ready."

TWENTY-FIVE

They got within two days ride of Sacramento without further incident. If there was any more trouble coming their way, it was coming slowly—and at this point, they knew it was to come from Sacramento.

Although Clint's left arm was stiff, and his shoulder still stung, his ankle was a lot better. He was able to walk almost normally.

Along the way, in a town for a supply stop, Clint got the answer he'd been waiting for from Rick Hartman. It seemed that Hartman—in knowing Clint Adams well—had been able to predict the route Clint would take in getting to Sacramento. This upset Clint. As friendly as he and Hartman were, he didn't like being *that* predictable. (He'd find out later that Hartman had left his messages along *several* routes from Nevada to Sacramento.)

In any case Hartman's telegraph message confirmed that a man—a very wealthy and powerful man—named Andrew Wagner had died recently in Sacramento. Hartman had also found out that a will reading was to be performed fairly soon.

Clint had told Hammer about this, and the black man felt somewhat better about the possibility of actually getting paid what they had been promised. Both men, however, still felt that *something* was going on that they were unaware of.

So two days out of Sacramento they camped . . .

"How much longer?" Wagner asked over dinner—a meager affair because they were low on supplies. "Before we get to Sacramento, I mean."

"Couple of days," Hammer said.

"I've been thinking about that," Clint said.

"So have I."

"I'll do it," Clint said.

"No, I will," Hammer said.

"Do what?" Wagner asked.

"I can do it better than you can," Clint said. "I'll be less noticeable."

"You?" Hammer said. "You're the one they're waitin' for, or have you forgotten?"

"Do what?" Wagner asked, again.

"Maybe," Clint said, "but I doubt they know what I look like. They don't *have* to know what you look like."

"Is that a crack about me being big?" Hammer asked.

"Can you fellas tell me what you're talking about?" Wagner demanded.

"Being big . . ." Clint muttered. He looked at Wagner and said, "One of us has to ride ahead into Sacramento, making sure the way is clear. Also to get us a hotel without the three of us riding in together."

"*Also* just to look around in general," Hammer said. "*You* can't go for obvious reasons, but your friend here is being stubborn."

"*I'm* being stubborn?" Clint said. "Jack, you decide. Who would be more noticeable riding into Sacramento, me or this big black—"

"See?" Hammer said, cutting him off. "I always knew you hated me because I was bigger than you."

"Bigger?" Wagner said. "I don't understand that, Hammer, but you'd certainly be noticed because you're black."

"He knows that, Jack," Clint said. "You're just getting a taste of the famous Hammer sense of humor."

"Oh, I see," Wagner said. "I'm afraid I don't have much of a sense of humor."

"Maybe you *did*," Hammer said, "and you forgot."

Of course he was kidding but Wagner took the remark seriously.

"No," he said, shaking his head, "I don't think I ever had much of a sense of humor."

"I think you're right," Hammer said, giving Clint the eye.

"I'm going in, Hammer," Clint said. "You ride along with Jack."

"Sure, okay," Hammer said. "It ain't *my* fault I'm black, though."

Clint put his hand on Hammer's big shoulder and said, "I know that. *I* forgive you."

"That's big of you, little white man."

In the morning Clint took the last watch so he'd be awake already when first light came. He saddled his horse and woke Hammer when he was ready to go. Wagner woke also. Since that morning of the ambush he had been waking up faster.

"I'll make some coffee," Jack said.

While he did that Clint and Hammer talked.

"Be careful," Hammer said. "You know they'll be waiting for you."

"I know that," Clint said, "but they'll be waiting for all three of us to ride in together. This way I may be able to slip in unnoticed."

"That's more than I'd be able to do, huh?" Hammer said.

"I've been thinking about that," Clint said. "I wondered if it wouldn't be wise for you and Jack to go in separately."

"For me, maybe," Hammer said. "I mean, there *are* other black men, and I *might* be able to get into town without too much fuss, but not the kid. Hell, they'll all know what he looks like. I better stick with him."

"Yeah," Clint said, "I agree."

Over coffee Clint got geography lessons from Wagner. He learned where the Wagner home was, where his father's office was, where his father's lawyer's office was—which is where the will was to be read. He also got descriptions of Wagner's brother, stepmother, sister, as well as his father's attorney. Clint felt sure he'd be able to spot these people when the time came.

Wagner also picked out a hotel and gave Clint directions on how to get there. The young man's memory of the city seemed intact—at least, Clint *hoped* it was.

He mounted up in preparation to leaving and looked down at the other two men.

"You fellas be careful, now," he said, looking specifically at Hammer. "Keep an eye on your back trail."

"Just watch yourself," Hammer said. "We'll see you in a few days."

Clint shook hands with both men and said, "A few days." He looked at Wagner and said, "That'll get you there with two days to spare. You're going to make it, kid."

TWENTY-SIX

Clint stopped and stared at the road ahead of him. This was clearly the way into Sacramento, for anyone approaching the city from this direction. For just that reason it was also clearly *not* the way he should be taking into the city. The road would *have* to be covered, and even though he was riding in alone, he was bound to be stopped and at *least* questioned.

He backed Duke up and got off the road. His original intention now was to circle around and come at the city from a different direction, but he had only gone a few yards when he realized that was no good. If the road was covered and he bypassed it, then it would *still* be covered when Hammer and Wagner came this way. What he had to do was see if it *was* covered and *un*cover it.

He turned Duke again and this time he still stayed off the road, but rode parallel to it. He had only to ride for ten minutes before he saw them. He reined Duke in and dismounted. He patted the big gelding on the neck, speaking to him soothingly.

"Just stay here and stay quiet, big boy," he said. "I'll be back soon."

He didn't bother securing Duke's reins. The big gelding wouldn't move unless he had to, and if he *had* to Clint wanted him to be free enough to do it.

Clint continued on foot and quickly determined that three men had been dispatched to cover this road into the city. There was one man on his side of the road, and two on the opposite side. That worked to his advantage. He could tackle the single man first, then work on the pair.

He approached the man from behind, being as quiet as he could. The other thing that worked to his advantage is that these were probably *city* men— men who had grown up and lived in Sacramento or San Francisco for most of their lives. Even though this was the Far West, these men were more easterners than anything else. With westerners he would not have been able to sneak up behind them so easily.

Clint was almost upon the single man when he started to turn. Clint used the butt of his gun to club the man down, even though he hated to use the weapon that way. When the man was on the ground Clint stared down at him. He knew what he should do and what Hammer would do, but he couldn't bring himself to kill the man while he lay there unconscious. It just wasn't in him to kill a helpless man in cold blood. Of course, *that* wasn't in keeping with his vaunted reputation as a killer, was it?

He didn't care.

He hogtied the man and left him there.

He had to move farther down the road before he could cross over to approach the other men. This might be harder since there were two of them, but as it turned out that was not the case. Because there were two of them they were talking with each other. He didn't even have to be as quiet as he was for the first man; they would not have heard him, anyway.

He was on them before they knew it.

"Hey!" one said as Clint knocked the other one unconscious.

"Just stand easy," Clint said, covering the man with his gun. He bent over and lifted the fallen man's gun from his holster.

He saw the man's eyes flick to the other side of the road.

"Don't worry about your other friend," Clint said. "He's going to be asleep for a while."

"What's this all about?" the man demanded.

"You tell me," Clint said. "Take out your gun and drop it to the ground."

The man did so, and Clint said, "Kick it away."

The man did that, too. Clint could see from the look on his face that the man had no desire to try to be a hero.

"Talk to me," he said.

"About what?"

"What are you and your friends doing here?"

"Nothing," the man said, shrugging.

Clint took a step closer to the man and suddenly rapped him on the nose with the barrel of his gun.

"Hey!" the man said, grabbing his nose, which started to bleed. "That hurt!"

"It's going to hurt a lot more if you don't answer my questions."

"Okay, okay," the man said, his eyes leaking tears. "Whataya wanna know?"

"Who sent you here?"

"We was hired."

"By who?"

The man shrugged and said, "Just a man. He come into the bar we was at, saying he was looking for some men for some work. He told us what he wanted, and what he was paying, and we took the job."

"Which was?"

"What?"

"What was the job?"

"Oh, we was supposed to watch for three men riding together."

"How were you going to recognize the men?"

"One was a big black man," the man answered, "and we were given pictures of the other two."

"Who has the pictures?"

"Ray."

"Which one is Ray?"

"Oh, uh, the other one, across the road. That, uh, was Ray."

"It still is Ray," Clint said. "He's not dead."

"That mean you ain't gonna kill us?" the man asked.

"No," Clint said, "not unless I see you in Sacramento. Understand?"

"Sure, mister," the man said, "I understand."

"Did you get paid?"

"Half up front," the man said.

"Be satisfied with that," Clint said. "Your friend Ray is tied up across the road. Wait here for half an hour and then untie him. Are you listening to me?"

"Yessir."

"Good," Clint said. "Take the money you got paid and go someplace else."

"But . . . we live in Sacramento."

"Go away for a while," Clint said. "Come back in . . . two weeks. Got it? Two weeks. If I see you before then, I *will* kill you."

"Mister—"

Clint pointed the gun at the man's head and said, "Tell me you weren't supposed to kill me and my friends?"

"Hey," the man said, cringing, putting his hands up in front of him, "hey . . ."

"I *should* kill you," Clint said, suddenly angry. "How much did you get paid? A hundred each? Two hundred? To do what, backshoot three men?"

"Mister—" the man said, and now the tears in his eyes weren't from the rap on the nose, "Mister—please—"

"Two weeks," Clint said. "Understand?"

"Yeah, yeah, I understand!"

"Make your friends understand, too," Clint said, "because if I see one of them, I'm coming after you, too."

"Hey," the man protested, "that ain't fair."

Clint smiled and said, "Life's like that, friend. Get used to it."

Clint tied the man up, knowing that he'd get free eventually. He also felt sure that the man would do his best to convince his friends that they should leave Sacramento for a little while.

He took their guns with him across the road, where he picked up Ray's gun, as well. Ray was still sleeping like a baby. Clint went through his pockets and found the photographs. One was of Wagner, and one was of him. It was a photo of himself he had seen before, in newspapers. He had never liked it.

He pocketed both photos and walked back to where he had left Duke, taking the three guns with him. He'd drop them on the ground one by one, between here and Sacramento.

TWENTY-SEVEN

Clint followed Jack Wagner's directions to the hotel he had picked out and was surprised to find that it was located right on the tip of Sacramento's Chinatown. Clint had been to Sacramento once or twice, certainly not as often as he had been to San Francisco, so he didn't know the city all that well.

The hotel had its own livery, so he handed Duke over and went inside to register.

"I'm expecting some friends," he said to the clerk, "so I'll need to reserve two more rooms."

Because of the location of the hotel there was no problem in reserving two more rooms. Not centrally located, Clint doubted that the hotel was *ever* completely filled.

"Of course, sir," the clerk said. He was young, polite, and eager to please. Maybe he envisioned himself moving up the hotel ladder of success. What was the top rung? A job in a Portsmouth Square Hotel in San Francisco?

Clint signed the register with Smith, Jones, and Brown. The clerk barely looked at the names.

"I'll need extra keys for all the rooms," he said,

113

and so collected two keys for his own room, and
one for each of the other rooms.

"And when will your friends be arriving?" the
clerk asked.

"A couple of days," Clint said, "maybe three." He
had traveled straight through, and so had made it in
less than the two days he had originally anticipated.
He'd have plenty of time now to look around and
maybe even get some information on the death of
Jack Wagner's father.

"Welcome to the Grand Star Hotel, sir," the clerk
said.

Clint had seen the star outside the hotel, but
hadn't realized that was the name of the place.

"Uh, thank you. Could I get a bath?"

"Certainly, sir," the man said. "When?"

"How about in ten minutes?"

"I'll have it ready, sir."

"Fine. Uh, how is your dining room?"

"Frankly speaking, sir?"

"I'd appreciate it," Clint said.

The man leaned forward like he was imparting a
state secret and said, "It's better than most of the
big hotels in the city."

"Really?" Clint said. "I'll have to give it a try."

"I think you'll be pleasantly surprised, sir," the
man said.

Clint hoped so. Wagner was a good cook, but trail
fare still couldn't compare with a good restaurant
meal.

Clint took his saddlebags and rifle up to his room.
After that he took a bath. Once he was freshened
up he went to the dining room to see how honest
the clerk had been with him. He was pleasantly

surprised to find that the man had not only been honest, but right. The food was very good, as was the coffee—which for Clint Adams was *more* than half the battle, right there.

After lunch he went out to the front desk to talk to the same clerk.

"I need a newspaper office," he said.

"Sir, I can have a boy go out and buy you a newspaper—" the clerk started, but Clint shook him off.

"No, you don't understand," Clint said. "I want to find a newspaper *office*. I need to look at some back issues."

"How far back?"

"Two or three months," Clint said.

"Well, all right. You'd probably want to go to the offices of the *Sacramento Union*," the clerk said, and proceeded to give Clint directions. "If you like you can walk there—it's a *long* walk—or I can have a boy get a cab for you out front."

"I'll take the cab," Clint said.

"Now?" the man asked.

"Yes," Clint said, "now."

TWENTY-EIGHT

At the offices of the *Sacramento Union* Clint went downstairs to the basement, where they had their morgue. He had received permission from the editor-in-chief to go through the back issues in the morgue by promising the man an exclusive interview before he left Sacramento. It was a lie. He didn't intend to give the man any kind of interview. He disliked most newspapers, and most newspapermen, and had no qualms about lying to them.

In the basement the attendant brought him a stack of papers and then asked, "What are you looking for?"

"Anything on Andrew Wagner," Clint said.

"He's dead," the attendant said. He was a thin, pale man who looked as if he *never* came up out of the basement. Judging from the way he looked he had been down there for about sixty years. Everything he touched bore the marks of his dirty, dusty fingerprints. When he said to Clint, "He's dead," he touched Clint's arm with one finger, leaving a dusty print behind.

"I know that," Clint said. "I want to read everything that was written about him *after* he died."

"Well, shit," the man said, "why didn't you just say that when you came in."

The man took a moment to look through the stack of papers he had just brought to Clint, then lifted the top half, set it aside, and removed the rest.

"In here?" Clint asked.

"That stack," the man said, indicating the stack he had set aside, "has everything that was written about the man after he was killed."

"Killed?"

"You said you knew he was dead," the morgue attendant said.

"What's your name?" Clint asked the man.

"Southern," the man said, "Mark Southern."

"Mark—can I call you Mark?"

"Everybody around here just calls me Dusty."

No wonder.

"Dusty, sit here for a minute."

The old man sat opposite Clint, leaning his bony elbows on the tabletop.

"I knew that Andrew Wagner had died," Clint said, "but I didn't know he'd been killed. What were the circumstances? Was he killed in an accident?"

"Shit no," Dusty said. "The man was murdered."

"You know that for a fact?"

"That's what the police said," Dusty said.

Clint touched the stack of papers and said, "I'm going to go through these, but you might be able to save me some time. How was he killed? Where was he killed?"

"He was found in an alley," Dusty said. "He'd been stabbed to death from behind."

Clint felt an unpleasant sensation in his stomach and said, "From behind?"

"That's right."

"Dusty," Clint said. "Where was he killed?"

"I don't know where he was killed," Dusty said, "but I know where he was found."

"Where was that?"

"Chinatown."

Dusty left Clint to go through the stack of papers, which Clint did, but thanks to Dusty it didn't take him quite as long as it might have.

As the morgue attendant had told him, the body of Andrew Wagner had been found in an alley in Chinatown. He had been stabbed three times in the back. The doctors said that any one of the wounds would have been fatal. Clint figured that someone had wanted to make damn sure that Andrew Wagner was dead.

No one knew what Wagner was doing in Chinatown—not his family, and not his business associates. As far as anyone knew, he had never even *been* to Chinatown before.

The papers carried the story for days, even weeks, after the fact. The *Union* followed the police investigation closely, and was constantly interviewing the man in charge, an Inspector West. The Inspector's nickname in the papers was "Handsome," because he was—obviously—so good-looking. In fact, the policeman got a lot of press because he was always seen squiring some of the more beautiful women of the Sacramento "upper crust."

Inspector "Handsome" West, Clint assumed, was an ambitious man. Such a man would have demanded to be in charge of the investigation just for its publicity value. Still, if he didn't solve the damned murder, the publicity just might hurt him more than it would help him.

The newspapers talked about Wagner's family, and even had photos. His wife, Lydia, was dark-haired and lovely. His daughter—Jack's sister, Donna—was also very pretty. His older son, Victor, was a dead ringer for Jack, only older. The paper also talked about his business associates, with his attorney, Daniel Forrester, getting most of the mention. There were no photos of Forrester, but he was described as being in his forties, and good-looking.

When Clint finished with the papers he called Dusty back over.

"Finished?"

"For now," Clint said.

"What did you find out?"

"Nothing you didn't already tell me," Clint said. "Tell me something, Dusty. What do you know about the other people involved."

"Like who?"

"The wife, Lydia."

"A bitch."

"The daughter, Donna?"

"Another bitch."

"They don't get along?"

"Nope," Dusty said, "in fact, they had to be pulled apart more than once in public."

"What about the son, Victor?"

"Useless."

"And the lawyer, Forrester?"

"A snake," Dusty said.

"In what way?"

"Folks say he and Mrs. Wagner were more than just friends," Dusty said. "Then again, they say the same thing about him and *Miss* Wagner."

"Hmm," Clint said, "maybe that's why the two women don't like each other."

"That could be one reason."

"What about the policeman in charge, West?"

"Handsome West has a reputation in this town," Dusty said.

"A good policeman?"

"A ladies' man," Dusty said, "and, yeah, he's probably a good policeman, but he's too busy trying to climb the social ladder to concentrate on his work."

"What about him and the Wagner women?"

"I'd be surprised if he hadn't been involved with one or both of them at some time or other."

Clint nodded and said, "Dusty, you've been a big help. Can I buy you a drink, or dinner?"

"Naw," Dusty said, "you gave me a chance to talk, and that's what I like to do. 'Sides, I hardly ever come up outta this place."

"Why not?"

"I don't like what goes on outside," Dusty said.

"Can't say I blame you for that," Clint said. "Thanks a lot."

He shook hands with the man and didn't wipe it afterward.

"Tell *me* something," Dusty called out as Clint started to leave.

"What?"

"You really the man they say you are?"

"Who is?" Clint said.

"That ain't a straight answer."

Clint stopped, turned around and said, "You're right. I'm a man like any other man, Dusty. I've killed some people along the way, I know my way around a gun, but *nobody's* the man the newspapers claim I am—and I sure as hell wouldn't want to be."

Dusty nodded and said, "Well, that's straight enough. You need anything else, you come and see me, hear?"

"I hear," Clint said, "and I'll do it."

TWENTY-NINE

After leaving the newspaper office Clint decided to walk back to his hotel. Along the way he came to a saloon and stopped in for a beer. He took a back table and did some thinking about the things he had found out, and what they meant to him and Hammer.

Hammer and he had hired on to get Jack Wagner to Sacramento safely, so he could collect his inheritance. The fact that Andrew Wagner had been *murdered* and had not merely died of natural causes should not mean anything to them. When Jack Wagner got to town and found out that his father had been murdered, it would be hard on him. Would it devastate him? Clint didn't know that, he didn't know the young man well enough to predict that. He didn't know what Jack would want to do, both before and after the reading of the will, but Hammer and Clint could very well leave Sacramento after the reading, and after they got paid.

Of course, *Jack* Wagner would have to live until the reading of the will, or they wouldn't get paid. So that in itself meant that there was more to their job than just *getting* him to Sacramento. They also had to keep him alive to collect his inheritance, and pay them. After *that* he could be killed, and it wouldn't affect them.

Wouldn't it?

Clint knew very well that he couldn't just leave Sacramento, knowing that Wagner might be killed at any moment. Whoever was trying to stop him from collecting his inheritance might not stop even *after* he had already collected it. And whoever was trying to stop him might very well be the same person—or persons—who were behind the murder of his father. That meant—to Clint's way of thinking, anyway—that in order to keep Jack Wagner alive, Clint was going to have to try to find out who killed his father.

He sat back shaking his head, staring at his half-empty beer mug. How could he expect to find out who the killer was when the police had been working on it for months without success?

Maybe what he had to do was go to see this Inspector West and tell him what had been going on. Maybe the information might somehow help the man in his investigation—if indeed he was even running a legitimate investigation. Of course, Clint wouldn't be able to discern that without meeting the man.

He finished his beer and left the saloon. His next move was to meet and talk to Inspector Handsome West. After that, he'd decide what he should do next.

Like anything in life, he was going to have to take this one single step at a time.

He caught a horsedrawn cab and told the man to take him to police headquarters.

"You just get into town?" the driver asked.

"That's right."

"You sure you want to go *there*?" the man asked. "There's lots of other places I could take you that would be more fun."

"I'm not looking for fun right now," Clint said. "Maybe I'll take you up on that later, though."

"Hey," the man said, "I'll be around."

The driver dropped him in front of a large stone building and said, "You want to look for that fun just ask for Lenny. People'll know where to get a hold of me."

Clint paid the man and said, "Thanks, Lenny."

"You ain't in some kind of trouble, are you?" Lenny asked.

"No, Lenny," Clint said, and as the cab pulled away he added to himself, "not yet, anyway."

THIRTY

Inside the building he presented himself at the big front desk and asked to see Inspector West.

"What's it about, sir?" the uniformed policeman behind the desk asked.

"It's about the Andrew Wagner murder."

The policeman leaned forward and asked, "What about it?"

"I may have some information about it for him," Clint said.

"Well," the man said, "you could give it to me—"

"I'd rather give it to him . . . thanks," Clint said.

The man leaned back and said, "All right, then. Have a seat and I'll tell him you're here. What's your name?"

"Clint Adams."

The man peered at him then and then said, "Uh, have a seat," again.

Clint sat on a straight wooden bench against the wall and waited. After about ten minutes an impeccably dressed man appeared and approached him. He was tall, in his forties, with dark hair streaked with gray. Clint could see where the man got his nickname from.

"Mr. Adams?" the man said, extending his hand.

Clint stood, accepted the hand and said, "That's right."

"A pleasure, sir," the Inspector said. "Your reputation precedes you. This is an honor."

"Inspector—"

"Oh, I'm sorry," the man said. "My name is Inspector Roland West. My friends call me Rollie."

"I thought your nickname was 'Handsome'?" Clint said.

West made a face and said, "That's a name that the newspapers stuck me with. It's not one I'm particularly fond of."

"Sounds like the same situation with me and my reputation."

West studied Clint for a moment and then said, "I'll keep that in mind. Would you like to come to my office?"

"Sure."

"This way, please."

He led him from the lobby into a hallway, down to the end where he allowed Clint to precede him into the office. He closed the door firmly and took his place behind his desk.

"Please," West said, "have a seat. Can I offer you something. Coffee, whiskey—"

"Nothing, thanks."

"I'm told you have some information about the murder of Andrew Wagner," West said. "Frankly, I can use all the information I can get."

"I don't know if what I have comes under the heading of information," Clint said. "It has to do with his son."

"Victor?"

"No, the other one," Clint said. "Jack."

"Jack?" West said, frowning. "Jack Wagner?"

"That's right," Clint said. "Andrew's younger son."

West stared at Clint for a few moments, then began to shake his head.

"I'm sorry," he said, then, "if Andrew Wagner had a son named Jack I didn't know anything about it."

"What?" Clint said, sitting forward in his chair. "Wait a minute . . . are you telling me that he *didn't* have a son named Jack?"

"That's what I'm telling you," West said.

"There's *no* Jack Wagner?"

"Mr. Adams," West said, patiently, "Andrew Wagner is survived by his second wife, Lydia, his son, Victor, and his daughter, Donna. Have you read his obituary?"

Clint felt like a fool. He *hadn't* read the man's obituary. He'd read everything else written about the man, but not that.

"Jesus . . ." he said.

"Mr. Adams," West said, "do you want to tell me what this is all about?"

"Yes, Inspector," Clint said, "I'd like very much to tell you all about it."

Inspector Roland West listened intently to Clint Adams's story about the young man with amnesia who hired him and his friend, Hammer, to get him to Sacramento safely. The young man claimed to be Jack Wagner, son of Andrew Wagner.

"Let me get this all straight," West said. "There actually *were* attempts on this young man's life?"

"Yes," Clint said, "two . . . and then on my way into the city I found three men waiting on the road along the way. They had these."

He handed the photos of himself and the man he knew as "Jack Wagner" across to the policeman, who took them and looked at them.

"This is curious," West said, "and I don't really know how it fits into my investigation, but it must."

"I'm worried about my friend, now," Clint said.

"I don't blame you," West said, handing the photos back. "Did you ask these men who hired them?"

"Yes, they were approached in a bar by a man."

"Naturally, they didn't ask the man for his name," West said.

"Not when he showed them cash."

"Of course not," West said. "Mr. Adams, where are you staying?"

"At the Grand Star Hotel."

The man frowned.

"On the edge of Chinatown?"

"That's right."

"Why there?"

"Jack Wagner suggested it."

"Andrew Wagner was killed in Chinatown."

"I know that."

"Curious," West said. "What will you do now?"

"I don't know," Clint said. "This throws me off completely. I guess I'll have to wait and see if this 'Jack Wagner' and my friend Hammer arrive in a couple of days. If they do, then it's easy. We'll just turn this fellow over to you so you can question him."

"Well," West said, "he hasn't committed any

crime, but I'd certainly like to question him."

"So would I," Clint said. "Inspector, would you mind if I talked to the family?"

West rubbed his jaw and said, "I guess that would be all right. I plan on talking to them again, myself. I'm afraid they might be getting tired of my face."

"I could come back and speak to you after I've talked to them," Clint said. "They might tell me something they haven't told you."

"That's certainly a possibility," West said. "I'd appreciate your cooperation on this, Mr. Adams."

"Clint."

"All right . . . Clint," West said. "I don't mind telling you I've run smack into a stone wall on this murder, and I don't like it one bit."

"I guess not."

West gave Clint a different look this time and said, "I suppose you took the time to do some research before you came to me?"

"I read some newspapers, yes."

"Then you no doubt know that I have a reputation as something of a . . . a . . ."

"Social climber?"

West smiled and said, "To put it simply, yes."

"I don't believe everything I hear or read about people, Inspector," Clint said. "Reputations are—"

"A dime a dozen?"

"Exactly."

"I guess we'd both do well to remember that—if we're going to work together on this, that is."

"I don't like being made a fool of," Clint said. "I'll do whatever I can to help you on this, Inspector."

"Rollie," West said.

"All right . . . Rollie."

Clint stood up, as did the policeman, and they shook hands.

"I'll get back to you as soon as I've spoken to the family."

"I could clear the way for you."

"I don't think that would be wise," Clint said. "They'd know then that we've already spoken. I'll get in to see them on my own."

"How will you do that?"

Clint thought a moment, and then asked, "Can you tell me where the Wagners are most likely to show up in the evenings?"

West smiled and said, "I can give you quite a few places . . ."

THIRTY-ONE

When Clint left the police station he found himself another cab and gave him the address of the Wagner offices. When he arrived he found himself standing in front of a three-story brick building. On the third floor was a large, plate-glass window with the legend: ANDREW WAGNER & ASSOCIATES. He wondered how Victor Wagner liked being lumped in with the "Associates." Then again, he knew nothing about the real Victor Wagner, only what the fake Jack Wagner had told him, and there was no way he could put any credence in *that* now, was there?

He went upstairs to the third floor and presented himself to the secretary on duty there. She was a handsome woman in her forties, crisp and efficient. She informed him that Mr. Wagner did not see anyone without an appointment, and there were *no* exceptions. He debated the wisdom of arguing with her, but decided not to. He really hadn't expected to get in to see the man, anyway. He just wanted to give it a try. He left, figuring that his only option now was to try and meet the Wagners—any *one* of them—in some sort of social situation.

• • •

After Clint Adams left his office Inspector West got hold of one of *his* officers—a man he could trust to do his bidding without question. He sent the man out to arrange a meeting for him later that afternoon.

Before returning to his hotel Clint stopped off again at the morgue of the *Sacramento Union*, just to take a look at Andrew Wagner's obit. Dusty dug it out for him and he read it. Sure enough it stated that Andrew Wagner was survived by his second wife, Lydia, his daughter, Donna, and his son, Victor. There was absolutely *no* mention of a son named Jack.

When Inspector Rollie West entered Delvecchio's Restaurant he spotted Victor Wagner seated at his table—or rather, what had been his *father's* regular table. Of course, it was now Victor's.

"Hello, Handsome," Victor said.

"Vic," West said, sitting opposite the man. A waiter appeared at his elbow immediately.

"Can I get you a drink, Inspector?"

"Yes, Sam," West said. "A brandy, please."

"Of course, sir."

Sam the waiter turned to Wagner, who dismissed him with a wave of his hand.

"To what do I owe the pleasure of buying you this lunch, Rollie," Wagner said.

West leaned back in his chair and regarded Victor Wagner across the table. Long ago he had decided that Victor was much easier to deal with than his father. While Victor looked a lot like his father, he had neither his father's backbone, or his business acumen. Indeed, Rollie West felt that he could play Victor Wagner like a finely tuned instrument.

"A man came to see me today."

"So?" Wagner asked. "What does that mean to me?"

"A lot," West said. "His name is Clint Adams."

"Should that name mean anything to me?"

"It should," West said. "He's otherwise known as the Gunsmith."

Wagner frowned. "That name rings a bell—"

"It should," West said. "The man is a goddamned legend."

Wagner gave him a bored look and said, "I don't believe in legends."

"Well, believe in this one," West said. "The man is bringing you trouble."

"How?"

West leaned forward and said, "He brought Jack Wagner with him."

Victor Wagner's lower jaw dropped and he said in a hushed tone, "Goddammit!"

"Exactly," West said, sitting back.

THIRTY-TWO

When Clint returned to the Grand Star Hotel the same clerk was on duty behind the desk.

"Are you the only one who works around here?" Clint asked him.

The man looked up, smiled, and said, "It only seems that way, sir. How did you like the dining room, by the way?"

"It was very good," Clint said. "Thanks for being honest."

"I'm always honest, sir," the man said, "it's just that so few people are willing to believe that."

"Well, I believe it," Clint said.

"I appreciate that, sir. Is there anything else I can do for you?"

"Yes, there is," Clint said. "Do you know a cab driver named Lenny?"

"Lenny?" the man said. "Well, yes, I do know him. Why do you ask?"

"I need to get a hold of him," Clint said.

"For tonight?"

"That's right," Clint said. "I need someone reliable to take me around to a few places this evening."

"Someone reliable," the man said. "And you want Lenny?"

"That's right."

"Sir, have you met Lenny?"

"Yes, this afternoon, when he drove me to the police station."

"The *police* station?"

"That's right. Is there something wrong with Lenny?" Clint asked.

"Well, sir . . ."

"Is he honest?"

"Honest?" the clerk said. "I don't know if *that's* quite the word I'd use for Lenny, sir."

"Reliable, then."

"Uh, yes, I think I can safely say that he's reliable . . . that is, if you're willing to pay enough."

"Well, I *need* someone reliable, and I'm willing to pay," Clint said. "Can you get him for me?"

"Sure," the clerk said, "I can get him."

"Good," Clint said, "have him here by eight. All right?"

"Yes, sir," the clerk said, "by eight."

Clint turned to leave, then turned back and said, "That is, unless you can think of some reason why I *shouldn't* use Lenny."

"Sir," the clerk said, "I'd be the last person to bad-mouth Lenny."

"Why is that?"

The man smiled and said, "He's my cousin."

When Clint exited the hotel at eight that evening Lenny was waiting for him out front.

"Hey, there!" Lenny said, dropping down from

the seat of his cab. "How did it go at the police station?"

"It went fine."

"It must've," Lenny said, "I see they let you out."

Lenny opened the door of his cab and allowed Clint to enter. The cab had a top, but it was not up at the moment.

"You want the top up?" Lenny asked. "You look like you're dressed for some high class places."

Clint had gone out earlier that evening and bought himself a new suit. If he was going to look for the Wagner family in the places the Inspector had suggested, he knew he'd need to be dressed properly.

"We don't need the top, Lenny," Clint said.

"Okay," Lenny said, "you're the boss."

Lenny climbed into his seat, then turned and looked down at Clint.

"I'm glad you asked for me, friend."

"I talked to the desk clerk here about you," Clint said.

"And he recommended me?" Lenny said, looking surprised.

"Well, no . . . but he didn't try to talk me out of it—even though he didn't seem to be very . . . enthusiastic about the idea."

Lenny grinned and said, "That's my cousin, Louis. He thinks I'm the black sheep of the family because I don't have a *real* job—but I tell you what. I'd rather be doin' this than what he's doin'. At least I'm my own boss, ya know?"

"Yes," Clint said, "I know."

"So where are we headin'?"

Clint rattled off the name of the three places Inspector West thought he might run into the Wagners this evening . . .

• • •

"To be frank," West had said, "you're more likely to run into Lydia than either Victor or Donna, but you never know what will happen. Donna likes to go out, er, sometimes."

"And Victor?"

"Victor is a bit of a workaholic."

"That's not the picture his brother—uh, the man who *claimed* to be his brother, painted of him."

"That man?" West said, indicating the photo in Clint's hand.

"Yes."

Before Clint left the Inspector's office the man said, "Why don't you let me have that photo. Maybe I can get the fellow identified."

"Why not?" Clint said, handing it back . . .

Now Clint wished he had the photo. He had the feeling that Lenny might have been more able to identify the man than anyone else in Sacramento.

"Hey," Lenny said, "you're gonna be mingling with the high and mighties tonight, ain't ya?"

"It's business, Lenny," Clint said, "just business."

"I don't know," Lenny said, "I just don't see you havin' business with those people."

"No? Why not?"

"Oh, I don't know," Lenny said. "You just look like the kinda fella *I* wouldn't wanna have business with, let alone those people. I wish I was a fly on the wall tonight. I think maybe you're gonna shake them up some tonight, yes sir."

Clint didn't bother telling Lenny that his intention was not to shake anyone up tonight, just to talk.

THIRTY-THREE

Lenny took Clint to the Alabaster House first. It was a large hotel and gambling casino. Clint spent one hour there and when he didn't see any of the Wagners, he went back outside to find Lenny lounging against his cab.

"See?" Lenny said. "Waiting right here, like I said I would."

"Good," Clint said. "You're reliable."

"Did my cousin Louis tell you that about me?" Lenny asked.

"Well, he said you *would* be reliable if you were paid enough to be," Clint said.

"And we ain't talked about money, have we?" Lenny asked.

"No, we haven't," Clint said. "Why is that, Lenny?"

" 'Cause I know you'll take care of me, that's why," Lenny said. Lenny opened the door to the cab so Clint could climb in.

"What's next?" Clint asked.

"The Belmont," Lenny said. "It's down the street a ways."

"Let's go."

On the way Lenny leaned back and asked, "Who are you lookin' for anyway?"

Clint didn't answer right away.

"Hey," Lenny said, "if you tell me I might be able to help you find them."

Clint thought it over, then decided to confide in the man.

"The Wagner family."

"All of them?"

"Any of them," Clint said.

"What do you want them for?"

"That's not part of the deal, Lenny," Clint said.

"No, it ain't," Lenny said. "All right, which one would you prefer?"

"Does it make a difference?"

"It does," Lenny said. "The son, Victor, you might find him at the Belmont, but if you want one of the, uh, ladies, we'll bypass the Belmont and go on to the Saratoga."

"Why is that?"

"The Belmont caters more to male tastes," Lenny said. "They got women available for, uh, well, they're available, if you get my meaning."

"I do."

"That leaves the Saratoga Hotel," Lenny said. "The young wife, Lydia, she likes it there."

"And the daughter?"

"She's been known to show up a night or two."

Clint thought a moment, then decided to go after one of the women. After all, he usually had better luck with women.

"All right, Lenny," Clint said, "let's go to the Saratoga."

"Right."

• • •

Victor Wagner was not keeping his mind on his gambling that night, or on the available women at the Belmont Club. He was more on the lookout for Clint Adams, who had been described to him in detail by Inspector West.

"I gave him the Alabaster, the Belmont, and the Saratoga," West said. "You wait for him at the Belmont."

"Why there?"

"Because," West said, patiently, "we have to pick one, and there's just more going on at the Belmont than at either of the other places."

"What am I supposed to do when he shows up?" Wagner asked.

"Talk to him," West said, "get him interested, and then take him to one of the back rooms. I'll have men waiting and watching. They'll take care of him."

"How much is this going to cost me, West?" Wagner asked.

"The going rate, Vic," West had replied, "just the going rate."

Wagner could see West's men circulating around, keeping their eye on him. He was the one who was going to make contact with Clint Adams, this "Gunsmith" West had told him about. He took out his handkerchief and mopped his sweating forehead, and then his mouth. He was nervous. He wasn't usually in a dangerous situation like this. West usually took care of everything.

Jesus, he thought, for my first time I have to draw some backwoods western legend?

He looked around and wondered where the hell

West was tonight. He might go to find West if there was no action here tonight.

Rollie West looked around the main casino of the Saratoga and saw Lydia Wagner standing at the craps table. Every time she leaned over to pick up the dice her breasts threatened to fall out of her low-cut gown—and she knew it! All of the men at the table had their tongues hanging out, waiting for it to happen.

Bitch, West thought. She knew how he felt about her, and she constantly flaunted herself in front of other men. It was bad enough he had to share her with her husband while the old man was alive. Now he had to watch while these other men salivated over her.

He wondered if Adams had gotten to the Belmont yet.

Outside the Saratoga Lenny's cab pulled up and he hopped down to open the door for Clint Adams.

"Impressive," Clint said, looking at the well-lit Saratoga Hotel.

"This is the place to be in Sacramento, Mr. Adams," Lenny said.

"Just make it Clint, Lenny."

"Uh, okay, Clint. Maybe there ain't as much goin' on here as there is at some of the other places," Lenny explained, "but you'll see more of the society types here than anywhere else."

"Like Lydia Wagner?"

"Yep," Lenny said, then he looked beyond Clint's right shoulder and said, "or Donna."

Clint turned and saw another cab pulling up

behind theirs. This one also had the top down, and
he could see the woman sitting inside. The driver
dropped down, opened the door, and helped her out.
She held her gown up as she stepped down, showing
a goodly length of well-turned calf and ankle. The
gown she wore was cut low, but she wore a shawl
around her shoulders so that all he saw at the
moment was a hint of cleavage. Her hair was piled
high on her head, with some ringlets hanging down,
and he could see that she had a lovely white neck.

"That's Donna Wagner?" he said.

"That's her."

"Jesus," he said, "the pictures in the newspapers
didn't do her justice."

Lenny shrugged and said, "Some people just don't
photograph well."

They watched as she mounted the front steps and
made her way to the entrance of the hotel.

"She's alone," Clint said.

"She usually comes alone," Lenny said, "but she
hardly ever leaves that way."

"Well," Clint said, "that's good news."

"Yeah," Lenny said, "I figure you got a *good* shot,
Clint."

"I'll take my best one," Clint said, and started up
the stairs himself.

Inspector Rollie West saw Donna Wagner walk in
the front door and shook his head. The stage was set
now for a genuine cat fight once Lydia and Donna
saw each other.

He watched Donna as she descended to the casino
floor, and he was just one of *many* men watching her. Donna was probably the only woman in

town who could steal some of Lydia's audience. That was why the two women hated each other so much—that and the fact that when Lydia married Andrew Wagner, Donna knew she'd end up sharing her father's fortune with the other woman.

West was intent on watching Donna *and* Lydia, waiting for the sparks to fly when they saw each other—*so* intent, as a matter of fact, that he almost missed the man who entered right behind her.

Clint Adams.

"Shit," he said, beneath his breath.

THIRTY-FOUR

Something had gone wrong.

Either Adams had managed to get away from the trap they'd laid for him at the Belmont, or he had never *gone* to the Belmont at all.

West cursed himself. He should have given Adams the name of the Belmont, and none of the others. This was his own fault, and he was going to have to take care of it.

Clint followed Donna Wagner down the steps to the casino floor and knew that he was going to be virtually unnoticed—by the men in the room, that is. He caught a few of the women watching him, but he knew it was only because he was fresh meat. If any of them ever found out that he wasn't rich they'd probably lose interest in him, real quick.

There was so much going on that it was hard to focus on any one thing. Lydia Wagner could have been there somewhere, but he knew he'd never find her. In any case, he was probably better off with Donna. *Someone* had sent men after the phony Jack Wagner to kill him, and they had never figured on

Donna. He couldn't help still thinking of the man he knew as "Jack Wagner." If he *wasn't* a brother, why was someone trying to kill him? And if he *wasn't* a brother, did that necessarily mean that he wasn't *anybody*?

Maybe he could get some answers from Donna Wagner.

He was trying to figure out the best way of approaching her when the opportunity simply presented itself. From where he was he could see the situation developing, and knew from experience that if she got close enough to the action, she'd end up getting involved.

She was just too damned beautiful not to.

There were two men who were obviously out of their element. They should have been gambling in a saloon somewhere. Instead they were in one of the fanciest gambling establishments in Sacramento. They were loud, lewd, and probably had had too much to drink. When Donna Wagner walked past them, they couldn't help themselves.

"Hey, whoa, whoa, little filly," one of them said. They were dressed well, but did not wear the clothes well. Obviously, they had hit some kind of financial windfall that enabled them to buy new clothes and gamble there.

He reached out and grabbed Donna Wagner by the arm.

"Miller," the man said, "see what I see?"

Miller, the second man, eyed Donna Wagner up and down while she tried to free herself from the first man's grasp.

"She's a beauty, ain't she, Ed?"

"She sure is," Ed said.

"Let me go!" Donna Wagner said.

"Take it easy, missy," Ed said. "We're just lookin' for somebody to have a good time with."

"Well, look for someone else."

"I don't think so," Ed said, smiling at Miller. "She's the one, huh, Miller?"

"Yup."

"Hey," Clint heard another man say, "let her go." The man who appeared was Victor Wagner, and his sister looked at him imploringly.

"Vic, make him let me go," she said.

Ed, the man holding her, was a big man, both tall and broad. He smiled evilly at Victor Wagner.

"Yeah, Vic," he said, tauntingly, "make me."

"I said let her go," Victor said, reaching for Ed's hand. Before he could grab it, though, Miller stepped in and hit him a crunching blow to the side of the head. Miller was almost as big as Ed, and the blow drove Victor Wagner to his knees. As Ed laughed, Donna gasped and Miller stepped in for another blow, Clint moved. He took three quick steps and caught the man's arm as he drew it back.

"Hey," Miller said. Clint pulled back on his arm, yanking the man off balance, then stuck out his foot so that the man tripped over it and fell.

"Hey," Ed said. Clint could tell they spent a lot of time together.

"Let her go," Clint said.

"Who says?"

"I do," Clint said, feeling like a ten year old.

Ed tightened his grip until Donna cried out. Clint reached out and closed his hand over the man's bicep, digging his thumb right into it.

"Hey," he said again, but he released the hold he had on Donna's arm. His arm hung down at his side.

"Go ahead," Clint said, "try something. You still have one arm left."

Ed glared at Clint, and then switched his glare to Miller, who had gotten back to his feet. Before either man could make a decision about what they would do several men surrounded them, grabbed them, and escorted them to the door . . . and out.

"Are you all right?" Clint asked Donna.

"Fine," she said, rubbing her forearm. "Thanks to you."

Victor Wagner regained his feet and was cleaning himself off.

"How about you?" Clint asked. "You okay?"

Wagner glared at Clint and said, "I didn't need your help," and walked away.

"Well, he's not a new friend," Clint said. He looked at Donna Wagner and asked, "What about you?"

"What about me?" she asked.

"Are you a new friend?"

She looked him up and down appraisingly.

"*I* could be a new friend," a woman's voice said before she could answer.

Clint turned and saw Lydia Wagner standing there with her hands on her slender hips. Up close she had very pale, almost translucent skin, with full lips that were painted very red.

"Sorry, Lydia," Donna said, taking Clint's arm, "but he's already taken."

THIRTY-FIVE

"Would you like a drink," Donna asked him, "or are you intent on gambling tonight?"

"I'm not if you're not," he said.

"Fine."

She kept a tight hold on his arm and walked him to the hotel dining room, where they sat and ordered drinks. He ordered a whiskey and she a brandy.

"Who was the other lady?"

"My stepmother."

"Stepmother?" he said, as if surprised.

"Yes," she said.

"She looks so young."

"Two years older than me."

"Well," Clint said, "she didn't look *that* young."

Donna smiled at him then and said, "I think I'm going to like you." She was still rubbing her arm where Ed had held her.

"Is your arm all right?" he asked.

She stopped rubbing it and said, "It'll be fine."

The waiter came and set their drinks down.

"Who was the other man?" Clint asked. "A jealous lover?"

"Hardly," she said, "that was my brother."

"Oh," Clint said. "I'm sorry if I embarrassed him."

"You didn't," she said. "He embarrassed himself by trying to help me."

"At least he tried."

She smiled a sad smile and said, "He's just not equipped for *that* kind of action . . . while obviously you are. What's your name?"

"Clint Adams."

"Why are you in Sacramento, Clint Adams . . . aside from saving damsels in distress?"

"Just passing through," Clint said. He wasn't quite sure how he wanted to continue to play this. "Brother, stepmother," he said. "Any other family around tonight?"

"No," she said. "My father was killed several months ago."

"Oh," he said, "I'm sorry."

She sipped her brandy with a solemn look on her face. Clint felt that she must have really loved her father.

"No other family then?" he asked.

"No," she said, "no other family."

So the Inspector had been right. "Jack Wagner" was a phony.

"Unless you count—" she started, and then stopped.

"Count what?" he asked.

"Well, I have a half brother—sort of."

"Sort of?"

"Well . . . he's a bastard. My father had some . . . other women between my mother and Lydia—actually, while he was still married to my mother.

One of them gave birth to a child."

"I see," Clint said, "and you consider him your brother?"

"Well," she said, shrugging, "he is . . . sort of, isn't he?"

"I suppose," Clint said. "I mean, you *do* have the same father, right?"

"Right."

"Then that makes him your brother, right?"

"Right."

"What's his name?"

She looked across the table at him then, frowned, and set down her glass.

"Why do you ask?" she said.

"Just curious."

"You're *very* curious, aren't you?" she asked.

"No more or less than anyone else," he said, but she wasn't accepting it.

"More, I think," she said. "What's on your mind, Clint Adams? I mean, really. Why did you play hero?"

"I was there," he said, "and you seemed to need help."

"And you *just* happened to be there?" she asked. "Why do you want to know my bastard brother's name?"

"Look," he said, picking up his glass, "if you don't want to tell me—"

"I'll tell you," she said, "but you have to tell me why you want to know."

He studied her for a moment, then put his glass down and said, "All right, I'll tell you."

And he did.

● ● ●

"*That* was Clint Adams," Inspector West said to Victor Wagner.

"Which one?" Wagner asked.

"The one who helped you."

"And where were *you* when Donna needed help?" Wagner asked.

"I didn't want Adams to see me," West said.

"She could have gotten hurt—"

"Look, forget about that," West said. "We have to deal with—" He stopped short when Lydia Wagner came over and joined them.

"What are you two looking so intent about?" she asked, sliding her arm through West's. "You're both neglecting me."

"You didn't look neglected a moment ago, at the tables," West said to her.

"Oh, them?" she said. "They were just some boys wishing me good luck, darling." She looked at Victor, then up at West again. "What's going on?"

"Business, Lydia," Victor said. "Why don't you go and find some more boys to play with?"

Her nostrils flared, but she slid her arm from West's and glided away without saying another word.

"She doesn't like being spoken to like that," West said. "You'll pay for that."

"Forget about *her*," West said. "What were you going to say?"

"We have to deal with Adams," West said, "and then we'll have to deal with his friend, Hammer, and your brother."

"That *bastard* is no brother of mine," Victor said.

"Well, your father thought differently."

"It doesn't matter what my father thought," Victor

Wagner said. "He's gone. What matters is what *I* think . . . *and* what you are going to do about Adams, and the others."

"What would you like me to do, Victor?"

"Handle it, Rollie," Victor said. "I want you to handle it."

"I will," West said, "as I always do."

THIRTY-SIX

Donna Wagner listened intently as Clint spoke and then was silent for several moments after he had finished.

"So what's the story?" he asked, finally. "Do you or do you *not* have a brother named Jack Wagner?"

"Uh, well, I do, yes," she said. "He's the bastard brother I was telling you about."

"Which explains why he was not mentioned in the obituary," Clint said.

"Yes."

"Which is why West was able to lie to me," Clint said. "He knew I'd check the obituary and see that only one son was mentioned."

"But why did he lie to you in the first place?" she asked. "He knows about Jack."

"I was going to ask *you* that question," he said. "What does he have to gain?"

"I don't know."

Clint paused a moment and then said, "Let's try something else. Did you write to Jack and tell him about your father?"

"Yes."

"Did you tell him that he had an inheritance?"

"Yes."

"How did you know that?"

"A few weeks before my father was . . . killed, he told me that he had provided for Jack in his will."

"How did you feel about that?"

"I didn't have a problem with it."

"Did Lydia and Victor know?"

"I don't know."

"How would they have felt if they *did* know?" he asked.

"Jesus," she said, "they would have both been livid. They wouldn't have stood sharing my father's money with his bastard."

"Why doesn't it bother you?" he asked, then added quickly, "or is that a question I should ask later . . . or maybe not at all?"

"No," she said, "it's all right. I've thought a lot about Jack. Even though we have different mothers, I don't see that he's any less my father's son than I am his daughter."

"That's . . . amazing," Clint said, "I mean, that you could feel that way."

"It's not so amazing," she said. "Think about it. Because he's not my mother's son doesn't mean he's not my father's son. He's not as much my brother as Victor is, but what I said is still true. He has the same blood relationship to my father that I do— which is more than I can say for Lydia."

Clint pondered that for a moment and then said, "I guess you're right. Uh, let's get back to the matter at hand, though."

"Which is?"

"Who tried to have Jack killed?" he said. "Was it your brother, or your stepmother?"

"I think it was my stepmother," she said after a moment.

"Why?" he asked. "Because you dislike her? Because you *want* it to be her?"

"No," she said, then, "yes," and then, "no," again, before she paused to think it over.

"All right," she said, "I don't like my stepmother and I would like it to be her, but that's *not* why I picked her. I just don't think my brother has the guts to do it, or have it done."

"All right," Clint said, "that's fair . . . but what if your brother had help?"

"You mean Lydia?" she asked. "You think they did it together? That she *got* him to do it?"

"That's a possibility," he said, "but there's another."

"And what's that?"

"Inspector West?"

"Rollie West?" she asked in surprise.

"Is that so hard to believe?" he asked. "Everything I've learned about the man indicates that he has ambitions. Maybe he saw a chance to make some money, *and* get a hold on your brother."

"I guess it's possible," she said.

"And something else is possible, too," Clint said.

"What's that?"

"Your father."

"What about him?"

"What if West killed him, or had him killed?"

Her eyes widened.

"He's the police, for God's sake!"

"I know," Clint said, "but that doesn't mean he can't commit murder."

"But . . . if he was working with my brother," she

said, "that would mean that he knew . . . that Victor
knew about my father's murder . . . *beforehand*?"

"Not necessarily," Clint said. "West could have
acted on his own."

"Yes," she said, "but wouldn't Victor have known
about it after?"

"Probably."

She put her face in her hands for a moment, then
looked at him with glassy eyes and said, "I can't
believe this. I can't believe that *Victor* would . . ."

"I know it's a hard thing to accept," Clint said,
"and maybe I'm wrong, but West and your brother
just came into the room together."

She turned in her chair and looked at the two men
who had just entered the dining room. They were
standing just inside the entrance and were staring
at the two of them.

"Why don't they come over?" she asked.

"Maybe they're trying to decide what to do," Clint
said. "Maybe they're trying to figure out what you're
telling me."

She looked at Clint and said, "What could I be
telling you?"

"That there is a Jack Wagner," Clint said, "and
that he is your brother."

"So then West knows that you know he lied,"
she said.

"That's right."

"What does that mean?"

"Well," Clint said, "it probably means that I have
very little chance of getting out of this hotel alive."

"I wonder what she's telling him," Victor Wagner
said.

"She doesn't have to tell him much," West said, "just that there *is* a Jack Wagner, and that he *is* your father's son."

"*Bastard* son," Victor Wagner said.

"That doesn't matter," West said. "By now Clint Adams knows that I lied to him."

"So what do we do?" Wagner asked.

"We're going to have to eliminate him," West said. "I'll have to send for some men."

"Policemen?"

"No, you fool," West said, "not policemen. Keep an eye on them while I take care of it."

"West," Wagner said, grabbing the other man's arm. The police inspector stared at his hand until Victor Wagner removed it.

"What is it?" West asked.

"What about Donna?"

"What about her?"

"Well . . . if Adams knows that you lied, so does Donna."

"That's right."

"You're not going to . . . I mean, you wouldn't . . . hurt *her*, would you?"

West pulled Wagner out of the dining room into the foyer and pressed his face up against his.

"Grow up, Victor," he said. "You want me to lie to you? We're in this together, and I'll eliminate anyone who would keep me from getting what I want."

"W-what does that mean?" Victor asked.

"That means you better have a talk with your sister," West said. "If she stays out of my way, she'll be fine. You tell her that, Victor. *Make* her understand."

"Make her understand?" Victor Wagner said, laughing helplessly. "H-how can I make her understand that I'm working with the man who killed her—*our*—father?"

"I don't know, Victor. How can you?" West asked, and walked away.

THIRTY-SEVEN

"You're a total stranger," Donna Wagner said to Clint Adams. "Why should I even believe a word of what you're saying?"

"I don't know," Clint said. "I can't give you a good reason to believe me. I guess you'll have to find out yourself."

"I just can't believe this," she said.

Clint was about to say something else when he saw Victor Wagner reenter the room and start their way.

"Maybe your brother can tell you something that will help you make up your mind."

She turned in her seat, saw her brother as he approached her.

"Donna," Victor said, "come with me."

"Why?"

"I want you away from this man."

"Why?" she asked again. "Is what he's been telling me true?"

"What's he been telling you?" Victor asked.

"That you and Roland West are trying to have Jack Wagner killed . . . and that you may have had

159

something to do with Dad's death. Is it true, Victor?"

"I'll tell you what's true, Donna," Victor said. "If you stay around this man you're going to get hurt."

"Why is that, Wagner?" Clint asked. "Are you going to try to have me killed, too?"

When Wagner didn't answer Donna said, "Well? What's your answer, Victor?"

Instead of answering her Victor grabbed her by the arm and pulled her to her feet.

"Come with me, dammit!" he snapped. "I don't want you to get hurt."

"Let me go!" Donna said, trying to pull free of a man's grip for the second time that evening.

"Donna," Clint said, "you'd better go with him. If West went to get help there'll be some men coming after me pretty soon. Your brother's right about one thing. You *might* get hurt."

Donna stopped struggling and looked up at her brother with hurt eyes.

"It is true, isn't it?" Donna asked. "You sent someone after poor Jack?"

"Poor Jack?" Victor said. "*Poor* Jack was gonna come back here and take what was ours, Donna."

"What was ours, Victor?" Donna asked. "All we have coming is what Dad wanted us to have."

"I want more than that, Donna," Victor said. "I want more than just some crumbs, and I'm gonna get it."

"With the help of Rollie West?" she asked.

"West works for me," Wagner said, finally releasing her arm.

"I doubt that," Clint said.

"What do you have to say about it?" Victor demanded.

"You're not smart enough to have West working for you. More than likely it's the other way around."

"*You* say."

"Okay," Clint said, "then if West works for you, you told him to kill your father."

"Victor!" Donna said.

"I didn't!" Victor said. "He did that on his own!" The words were out of his mouth before he realized it.

"Then it is true," she said. "You knew!"

"No, no," Victor said, turning desperate now, "I didn't know before. You have to believe me, Donna. I only knew *after*."

"Then we have to tell the police," Donna said.

"What good would that do?" Victor asked.

"You'd be bringing your father's killer to justice, Wagner," Clint said, "and you'd probably still benefit from his death—and you wouldn't have to split it with West, would you?"

Victor Wagner seemed to think that over, but then he shook his head.

"No," he said, then, "West would kill me."

"He'd be in jail," Clint said.

"He'd have me killed even from there," Victor insisted.

Clint looked at Donna and said, "I guess we know who works for who, now, don't we?"

Donna looked at her brother with a mixture of pity and hatred.

"Come with me, Donna," her brother said. "Adams is not gonna get out of this hotel alive."

"I'm not going anywhere with you, Victor," she said. "I'll see you pay for what you've done—you *and* West."

"Don't you understand?" Victor asked. "If you stay with Adams, if you get in West's way, *you* won't get out of this hotel alive, either."

People from other tables were looking at them now, not sure what they were hearing.

"We're attracting a lot of attention, Wagner," Clint said. "Other people are listening. When West finds out that you've talked, what do you think *your* chances of getting out of this hotel alive will be?"

Victor frowned and shook his head.

"No, West and I are partners."

"A moment ago you said he worked for you," Clint said. "Your relationship is going downhill fast."

"One last time, Donna," Victor said, imploringly. "Come out of here with me. Get away from *him*!"

"I'd rather die with him," she said to her brother, "than leave here with you, Victor."

Victor Wagner's face turned ugly then and he took a couple of steps away from his sister.

"Have it your way, then!" He turned on his heel and stalked out of the room.

Donna turned to Clint and said, "What do we do now?"

"Now," Clint said, "we have some cups of coffee."

When Victor Wagner came out of the hotel dining room he saw Inspector Roland West waiting for him. West had half a dozen hard-looking men with him— men who were obviously not policemen.

"Well, Victor?" West said.

"She—she won't leave him," Victor said.

"And what did you tell her, Victor? Hmm?"

Victor Wagner looked away, unable to meet Roland West's eyes.

"That's what I thought," West said. "All right, you," he said to one of his men, "stay with him. Make sure he doesn't go anywhere."

"Hey, Rollie—" Victor started.

"Shut up, Victor," West said. "Just shut up and you may live through this." West turned to his other five men and said, "You know who we want. He's not to get out of the hotel, understand?"

The men nodded.

"I don't want any commotion inside."

"What if he don't leave the dining room?" one man asked.

"He's got to leave sometime," West said, "and when he does, I want him. Do you understand?"

"You want him alive," the man asked, "or dead?"

"How much are you getting paid for this, Russell?" West asked.

"A lot," the man called Russell said.

"Then that answers your question," West said, "doesn't it?"

THIRTY-EIGHT

"Sit down, Donna;" Clint said, pouring her another cup of coffee.

"How can you just sit there?" she asked. "Men are coming here to kill you—and probably me, now."

"Not in here, though," he said. "As long as we stay in here, we're safe. Sit down."

She hesitated, and then sat.

"It's all true," she said, in disbelief.

"I've had some trouble telling the lies from the truth," Clint said, "but I think I've finally got it."

West joined forces with Victor Wagner, then tried to speed up Victor's rise to the top—and his own—by killing Andrew Wagner. Victor probably didn't know about it beforehand, and was too frightened—and greedy—to do anything about it afterward.

West probably sent the men to kill Jack Wagner to keep him from returning to collect any portion of his father's estate. He and Victor were probably willing to share with Lydia and Donna, but not with the bastard son.

"If I hadn't contacted Jack," Donna said, "West probably wouldn't have sent anyone after him."

"You did what you thought was right, Donna," Clint said. "You can't blame yourself for that."

"What I thought was right is going to get you, me, *and* Jack killed, Clint."

"Maybe," Clint said, "and maybe not."

"How can you say that?"

"All we have to do is get out of the hotel alive and get to the police."

"West *is* the police!"

"So we go to some honest policemen," Clint said. "There have to be some in this city, don't there?"

"I suppose," she said, "but how do we get out of here to find them?"

"We come up with a plan."

"Do you have one?" she asked.

"If I did," he said, "we wouldn't have to come up with one, would we?"

She smiled in spite of herself and said, "No, I guess we wouldn't."

"We're getting more company," Clint said.

She turned and saw Inspector Roland West walking toward them.

"What's he want?" she asked.

"Let's listen and find out."

When West reached the table he pulled out a chair and sat down without a word. The waiter saw him and came over to the table.

"Can I get you something, Inspector?" the man asked.

"Yes, bring another cup," West said. "I'll have some coffee."

"Right away."

As the waiter left the Inspector smiled and said, "People hereabouts know me."

"Not the way *we* know you," Clint said.

"We?" West said, looking at Donna. "Are you taking sides with this man against your family, my dear?"

"My family?" Donna asked. "I have no family left, thanks to you. You've perverted my brother Victor's mind, and you're having my brother Jack killed."

"How can you refer to that bastard as your brother, Donna? I can't understand that."

"And I can't explain it to you, Roland," she said. "A man like you would never understand."

The waiter returned with the empty cup and poured West a cup of coffee. West thanked him politely and drank from it as the man walked away.

"Donna," West said, "I'm giving you an opportunity to walk out of here with me right now."

"No."

"Don't decide too hastily, my dear," West said. "Think about it."

"I said no," she said. "I'll tell you the same thing I told Victor. I'd rather die with Clint Adams than walk out of here with you."

"You *will* die with him, Donna," West said. "I'm too close to what I want to let that deter me."

"Go with him, Donna," Clint said.

"What?" she gasped.

"There's no point in your dying, too."

"He's going to kill me anyway, Clint," Donna said. "Sooner or later he'll have to." She looked at West and said, "He knows it and I know it."

"Not really, Donna," he said. "You can't prove anything, and it would be your word against mine—and don't forget who I am."

"A hateful, disgusting man is what you are, Rollie West," Donna said. "It makes my skin crawl just to be near you."

That seemed to offend West, which Clint found funny.

"I'm sorry you feel that way, Donna," West said. He looked at Clint and said, "You have to leave this hotel sometime, Adams. I'll be waiting."

"Why?"

West frowned and asked, "Why what?"

"Why do I have to leave?" Clint asked. "I can get a room here, there's plenty of food and drink, and even some gambling. I can be quite comfortable here for a *long* time, West. If you want me I'm afraid you're going to have to come in and get me."

West regarded Clint for a few moments, then leaned toward him and said, "If that's what I have to do, Adams, I'll do it."

"Then do it, West," Clint said. "Come on. I'm waiting for you—I'm waiting for *you*. Send your men in. When I'm finished with them I'll be coming for *you*. That's something for you to think about."

West stared at Clint for a few moments, then stood up and stiffly walked to the door.

"You frightened him," Donna said. "You actually *scared* him, Clint. I've never seen the great Rollie West frightened."

"Yeah," Clint said, "maybe, but even if I did that's not necessarily a good thing."

"Why not?"

"Because frightened men are unpredictable, Donna," Clint said, "they're *very* unpredictable."

"So what are we supposed to do now?"

"We're still trying to come up with a plan," he said.

When West walked back outside, his six men and Victor Wagner looked at him expectantly. There was someone else there too, though, someone Roland West had not expected.

"Do you have a problem, Rollie?" Lydia Wagner asked.

THIRTY-NINE

Lydia Essex Wagner had spent most of her twenty-seven years controlling men. From the age of fourteen she had found it very easy—and it had become progressively easier as the years passed.

Andrew Wagner had been easy. He had been very lonely, and had succumbed to her beauty even before they actually met. She knew the instant that they met that she would be able to get him to marry her.

Once they were married she realized that Victor Wagner was very unlike his father. He was not as strong or intelligent, but he was younger and better looking. He would also be even *easier* to control than his father—and she had been right.

For a long time Lydia had been fencing with Rollie West. She waited before she actually slept with him, and then she did that just once, to give him just a taste and keep him interested.

Now it was time to go all the way with him.

"Lydia," West said, "you don't belong here."

"Like hell I don't," she said. "I set this whole thing up, Rollie."

"What are you talking about?" he asked.

She took his arm and led him away from the others, so that only he could hear her.

"Who do you think told Victor to go to you?" she asked him. "Who do you think got him to do everything you told him to do?"

West looked at her and said, "You?"

"If it wasn't for me," she said, "Andrew would still be here, and we'd all still be on the outside looking in."

West stared at her, then said, "Lydia." There was admiration in his tone. "We really are two of a kind, aren't we?"

"Never mind that," she said. "You have a problem now, I can see that. What is it?"

So he explained to her about Jack Wagner still being alive and hiring Clint Adams, and about Adams coming to Sacramento and asking questions. He also told her what the situation was at the moment.

"He came right to you, Rollie," she said. "All you had to do was take care of him."

"I tried," he said.

"You didn't try hard enough."

"I'll take care of him now."

"When? When he leaves the hotel? He's right, you know. He can stay in there forever."

"I can't touch him in there, Lydia."

"Why the hell not?" she asked. He was taken aback by her tone, and her language. "Rollie, what are you worried about?"

"I can't just kill him in front of witnesses," he said. "My job, my reputation—"

"Rollie, Rollie," she said, putting her hands on his

arms, "think about it. Adams will be dead. So will Donna. When Jack arrives you'll take care of him. That will leave only Victor and me as heirs," she explained, looking over at Victor. "Does that give you any ideas?"

West looked at Victor too, then at Lydia Wagner's eyes, mouth, and pale skin.

"Yes," he said. "Victor is weak, he'll be a liability."

"Yes," she said, rubbing his arms, "and then there will be only me . . . and you, of course."

He stared at her and said, "Of course."

"What will you need with your job, then?" she asked.

Abruptly, he grabbed her by the upper arms. He was holding her so tightly that her circulation was cut off.

"Rollie!"

"If you think you can play me for a fool, Lydia, the way you did the Wagner men, think again," he said. "After I've taken care of all of this it *will* be just you and me."

"Of course it will, darling," she said.

He released her arms then, and rubbed the redness he had left where he held them.

"Go into the casino," he told her, "and wait there for me."

"Yes, darling," she said. "Roland . . . be careful."

"I'll be very careful, Lydia," he promised. "I wouldn't want to get killed, because then you'd have to find someone else to do your dirty work, wouldn't you?"

He watched her walk away, then went back to where his men were waiting.

"What do we do, boss?" Russell asked.

"We're going to take him inside the hotel," West said.

"We're gonna kill him in front of witnesses?" Russell asked.

"You'll all be covered," West said. "I'll protect you. I'll simply tell the story that I tried to arrest him, he resisted, and you all helped me capture him. Unfortunately, he'll be killed."

"Can you do that?"

"Of course I can, Russell," West said. "I can do that, *and* pay you well. Are you with me?"

Russell looked at the other men, then turned to West and said, "We're with you, boss."

FORTY

Inside the dining room the coffee pot ran dry. The waiter came over and asked, "Another pot, Miss Wagner?"

"No, Maurice," she said. "We're finished. Please put the bill on my tab."

"As you wish," Maurice said, and backed away.

"Well?" she asked Clint. "Do you have a plan?"

"Yes," he said.

"What is it?"

"Staying alive," he said.

"But *how*?"

He looked around and saw the door Maurice had gone through.

"Does that lead to the kitchen?"

"Yes."

He stood up and said, "That's where we're going."

"What are we going to do in there?" she asked as he took her hand and pulled her from her seat.

"Find someplace for you to hide until this is all over."

"I can just go back to the casino," she said.

"You'd never make it," he said, "at least not

173

through the front way. Is there a way to get there through the kitchen?"

"I don't know," she said.

"Well then," he said, "let's ask Maurice."

As they crossed the floor toward the kitchen the other diners watched them curiously. The looks they got were even more curious when they actually *entered* the kitchen.

Stan Russell entered the dining room just as Clint and Donna were going into the kitchen. Russell knew that if he pulled this off he'd be in line for a lot of money, and maybe a job with the Wagner family. He wasn't about to let that slip from his grasp.

"They went into the kitchen!" Russell said to the men outside the dining room, including West.

"Take care of them, Russell," West said. "I'll be in the casino."

"Miss Wagner?" Maurice asked, in surprise. "Was there something else?"

"Is there a way Miss Wagner can get to the casino floor from here, Maurice?" Clint asked.

"Why, yes," Maurice said, "there's another door."

Clint looked out the window of the kitchen door and saw three men crossing the dining room. None of them was West, but that didn't matter. He knew they *worked* for West.

"Take her to that door, Maurice," Clint said, "and go out yourself."

"What? I can't, I have to—"

"And take the rest of these people," Clint said,

indicating the cooks and other waiters.

"Sir, I don't see how—"

Clint drew his gun and said, "Now, Maurice!"

Maurice grabbed Donna's arm and pulled her across the kitchen, shouting at the others as he went.

Donna turned and called out to Clint, "Be careful."

And then he was alone in the kitchen.

Russell and two of his men reached the kitchen door and stopped. One of them peered through the window.

"It looks empty," the man reported to Russell.

"Good," Russell said, "less witnesses to deal with. We're goin' in, boys. This means a lot of money to us, so let's not mess it up."

As the swinging door opened Clint forced himself to wait until the three men were all inside. He was holding a pot of boiling soup, and he could feel the heat even through the towels he was holding it with. He forced himself not to think about what the soup would do to the men's skin. As the swinging door closed behind them he threw the entire contents of the pot at them.

Russell saw it coming, and was the only one who was able to cover up in time. He crossed both arms across his face as the hot liquid hit them. The other two men screamed. Russell cried out, too, but he was not in the same pain as the others. The flesh of their faces burned like fire and they forgot all about Clint Adams.

Russell dropped his hands, pressed them to the small of each man's back and pushed them toward Clint Adams. Behind them he raised his gun . . .

As Clint saw the two men stumbling toward him he knew they were no danger to him. The flesh of their faces had already turned red and begun to blister. He lofted the empty soup pot over their heads and drew his gun.

Russell saw the soup pot coming toward him. Even as he side-stepped it, he knew that he had cost himself just a split second—which was enough time for Clint Adams.

Clint fired.

FORTY-ONE

Clint checked the man he'd shot to make sure he was dead. He then moved to the other two men, who were writhing in pain on the floor. He knocked one of them unconscious, and then bent over the other one, taking him by the front of the shirt.

"Now you're going to answer some questions," he said, "or you won't be getting any medical help . . ."

From the casino floor neither Lydia Wagner, Donna Wagner, Victor Wagner, nor Roland West heard the shot. They were too busy eyeing each other across the crowded room.

It suited West that Donna was in the casino. There he could keep an eye on her.

Donna felt the same way about him, although most of the time she was glaring at her brother—something that did not escape the notice of Lydia.

For his part Victor could not meet the gaze of any of the other three.

After the man told Clint that there were two other men waiting for him, he knocked him unconscious as well. The man's face was beginning to resemble overdone meat. Clint didn't think there was anything that a doctor could have done for him. It might have been kinder for him to have killed them both.

He knew now that the other two men would be waiting for him by the back door, the one Maurice had taken Donna through, so Clint went out the front. He could have gone around to face the other two men and taken care of them, but he decided to go right for West. Once he took care of the man paying them, the others wouldn't be a problem.

He went directly to the casino.

West couldn't believe his eyes when he saw Clint enter the casino.

"Damn!" he muttered under his breath. *Five men* and they couldn't take care of him?

Lydia saw Clint and watched him coolly. Even if Adams was the eventual winner of this confrontation he was, after all, just another man.

When Donna saw Clint her stomach jumped. What would happen now, right here on the crowded casino floor?

Victor saw Clint and stopped in his tracks. Would the man come after him? No, he was heading for West.

Maybe they'd kill each other . . . or was that too much to ask?

When Clint reached West he could see the tension in the man's body. West's face, however, appeared calm.

"You're resourceful," West said. "You took care of all five men?"

"It's just you and me now, West."

"What can you do here, Adams?"

"Kill you, if you don't do as I say."

West laughed.

"You think you can get away with killing a policeman?" the Inspector asked.

"A crooked policeman, yes."

"Who'd believe you?" West asked.

"Look over there, Inspector," Clint said, inclining his head.

West looked and saw that the three Wagners—Lydia, Donna, and Victor—had united across the room and were watching him.

"They're family, Inspector," Clint said, "you are not. They are also a *prominent* family in this city. I think with their backing I won't have any trouble."

"What makes you think they'll back you?" West asked.

"Donna certainly will, don't you think?" Clint asked. He could see by the look on West's face that the man *did* agree. "And Victor, I think he'd like to be out from under your thumb. And Lydia . . . well, you tell me about Lydia."

West looked over at Lydia, who had her arm through Victor's.

"Lydia," West said, his tone dead, "will do what's right for Lydia."

"That's right," Clint said. "Now you have two choices, Inspector. Either hand me your gun, or make a move for it."

West looked at Clint and said, "Come now, Adams, this is not the wild, wild West."

The man's hand went inside his coat very slowly and came out with his gun, which he handed to Clint.

"We'll see who believes who," West said.

Clint could see that the man was unsure of himself, though, and as he tucked the policeman's gun away in his belt he said, "Yes, we'll see."

FORTY-TWO

Donna Wagner sat astride Clint Adams and rode him slowly, moving up and down the length of his shaft easily, lovingly. Her hands were braced on his chest and his hands were cupping her ass as she continued to move on him.

She leaned over so he could mouth her breasts, kissing them, sucking the nipples. He released her buttocks so he could fondle her breasts with his hands, holding them to his mouth now, and she moaned as he worked on her nipples with his tongue, lips, and teeth.

"Oh, God," she said as her belly started to tremble. She began to rise and fall on him faster, coming down harder and harder each time and even twisting her butt a bit. Abruptly she fell atop him, pressing herself to him, and he cupped her buttocks again as he felt the surge building up inside of himself.

"Oh, yes," Donna began to mutter into his ear, the words tumbling out together, "yes, yes, yes . . ."

"Yes!" Clint roared and then they were bucking against each other, the bed making little jumps off the floor. His arms were around her, holding him to her while waves of pleasure washed over both of them, and her teeth were in his shoulder as she sought to smother a scream . . .

Later they lay together in his bed, in his hotel room, and discussed the events of the night before, and what the backlash would be.

"Rollie West is in trouble," Donna said. "My family name was enough to convince his superiors that he should be investigated. Even if they don't get him for killing my father, or planning it, there have to be a lot of other dirty activities that he was involved in."

"I would think so," Clint said. "What about your brother?"

"My brother," she said, her voice sad. "Victor will no longer be involved with the family business. We talked about it last night. He will also give up whatever my father left to him in his will."

"If there's anything to give up," Clint said.

"What do you mean?"

"Your father was a smart man, Donna," Clint said. "Do you think he didn't know what his son was?"

"I hope he did," she said.

"And Lydia?"

Donna sighed and said, "Lydia is Lydia. We can't even cast any suspicion on her, so she'll go on doing what she does best."

"Talk to Victor some more," Clint said. "He might be able to give you something you can use on her."

"Do you think so?" she asked.

"It's worth a try," he said. "In any case, I guess this puts you in control."

"When will Jack and your friend be here?"

"Probably tomorrow."

She ran her hand over his chest, then down over his belly.

"I hope I can get Jack to stay and help me," she said.

"I hope he has the rest of his memory back," Clint said. "There are still some unanswered questions."

"Like what?"

"Like who killed those first three men who tried to kill him?" Clint said. "Your half-brother has already proven to me how inept he is with a handgun, and almost as much with a rifle."

"Jack?" she said. "Jack's an excellent shot."

"Is he?" Clint asked. He remembered the shot Jack had made in saving him on that ridge. It *could* have been a lucky shot, or it could have been a fine shot fired from some lost memory.

"With a rifle and a pistol," she said. "He's not *fast* or anything, the way you are, but he's an excellent shot."

"Well," Clint said, "I guess we'll have to wait and see if we'll ever get the whole story."

"As long as he's still Jack," she said, "he can help."

Her hand closed over his semi-erect penis and she began to fondle him. He moved his hips and moaned in appreciation.

"And what about you?" she asked.

"What about me?"

"How long will you be here to help me?" she asked.

"Not very long," he admitted. "Your brother will pay us what he owes us and we'll probably be on our way."

"Well, in that case," she said, sliding one leg over him, "I have something you can help me with right now."

He slid his hand down her thigh, over her buttocks, along the crease between the two lovely cheeks, reaching further and further until his middle finger was wet from her.

"Let's get to it, then," he said.

Watch for

OUTLAW WOMEN

134th novel in the exciting GUNSMITH series
from Jove

Coming in February!

If you enjoyed this book, subscribe now and get...

TWO FREE

A $7.00 VALUE–

If you would like to read more of the very best, most exciting, adventurous, action-packed Westerns being published today, you'll want to subscribe to True Value's Western Home Subscription Service.

Each month the editors of True Value will select the 6 very best Westerns from America's leading publishers for special readers like you. You'll be able to preview these new titles as soon as they are published, *FREE* for ten days with no obligation!

TWO FREE BOOKS

When you subscribe, we'll send you your first month's shipment of the newest and best 6 Westerns for you to preview. With your first shipment, two of these books will be yours as our introductory gift to you absolutely *FREE* (a $7.00 value), regardless of what you decide to do. If

you like them, as much as we think you will, keep all six books but pay for just 4 at the low subscriber rate of just $2.75 each. If you decide to return them, keep 2 of the titles as our gift. No obligation.

Special Subscriber Savings

When you become a True Value subscriber you'll save money several ways. First, all regular monthly selections will be billed at the low subscriber price of just $2.75 each. That's at least a savings of $4.50 each month below the publishers price. Second, there is never any shipping, handling or other hidden charges—*Free home delivery*. What's more there is no minimum number of books you must buy, you may return any selection for full credit and you can cancel your subscription at any time. A TRUE VALUE!

J.R. ROBERTS
THE
GUNSMITH